"Gr[...]
she he[...]
When [...] [...] [...] [...] [...]
surprised. Mr. Benson's face did not look like
that of a winning coach's. "Yes, but this was an
easy meet. The next ones will be tougher," he
said.

"We'll beat everyone!" Casey told him
confidently.

"Don't be so cocky," Bear admonished her.
"We're not guaranteed to win anything,
considering the way you performed today."

"What?" Casey dropped her fork. "But I won
the beam and finished second All-Around."

"Maybe so, but you're still not working up to
your ability. You'd think after all these years,
you'd be able to concentrate," he commented.

"Concentrate!" Casey jumped to her feet.
"How can I concentrate when you're always
picking on me? Why don't you just leave me
alone!"

Other Fawcett Girls Only Titles:

Casey and the Coach

PERFECT 10
1

HOLLY SIMPSON

FAWCETT GIRLS ONLY • NEW YORK

RL1: $\dfrac{\text{VL 6 \& up}}{\text{IL 7 \&up}}$

A Fawcett Girls Only Book
Published by Ballantine Books
Copyright © 1989 by Cloverdale Press, Inc.

Library of Congress Catalog Card Number: 89-91169

ISBN 0-449-14589-1

Manufactured in the United States of America

First Edition: August 1989

To
my daughters,
Kelly, Kari, and Kristy O'Connell,
who added so much to this book

Chapter 1

* * * * * * * * * *

S<small>MACK</small>!

Casey Benson crashed onto the mat under the balance beam. Closing her eyes, she sighed. She *had* to add this new move to her routine if she was going to make Elite.

The Flyaway Gym Club in Fairfield, Illinois, was almost empty as she climbed back on the beam for the hundredth time that day. Only it seemed like a thousand. She had to get it right—at least once before going home.

Knowing timing was crucial, Casey concentrated hard before throwing herself into a back handspring. As she landed on the beam, she knew there wasn't enough momentum to go into the second half of the combination. She felt herself start to fall. For an instant she flailed helplessly and then, once again, fell onto the crash pad below. Lying exhausted beside the beam, staring up at the high ceiling of the gym, she wondered if she had what it took to be a national-level gymnast. After ten years of training, fourteen-year-old Katherine Corinne Benson, known as K.C. or Casey to her family and friends, still had doubts. Was she really good enough?

And was the effort worth it?

Casey's goal of going Elite took all her free time and kept her from participating in other things at school. She missed a lot of the fun at Prescott Junior High because she never had time to just hang out with her friends—except for Jo and Monica, who also worked out at Flyaway.

Casey saw her coach, Chip Martin, looking down at her as she lay on the mat. "I think I'm dead," she announced, closing her eyes.

Chip leaned on the end of the beam. He laughed and shook his head. "Come on, funny girl. Open up those pretty blue eyes and try it again."

I always could make him laugh, Casey thought. Making people see the funny side of things seemed to come easily to her, and with Chip, it eased the tension that built up in a daily five-hour practice.

Opening her eyes, she stuck out her tongue at him. He laughed again, and she noticed how many crinkly lines he had in the corners of his eyes. His straw-colored hair stuck out from underneath the Chicago Cubs baseball cap he wore to workouts— mostly to keep his wiry hair from springing up all over his head.

"Give me a break," Casey moaned. "How can you possibly know I'm not dead when you're relaxing up there and *I'm* the one who munched."

Chip just grinned as Casey reluctantly stood up and pulled herself back onto the beam. She knew she would have to keep trying until she completed the move at least once. As much as Chip joked around, he could get pretty angry when someone wasn't putting out her best effort.

"Okay, slave driver." Casey got into position, determined to make it this time. Pushing everything out of her mind except the trick itself, she threw herself into the air. Landing solidly from the handspring, she knew she could go into the back somersault in layout position. She soared up and over the beam. The landing at the end was wobbly, but she did get both feet on the beam before jumping off.

"All right!" Casey said, giving Chip a high five.

"That's it for tonight, Champ." Chip ruffled her short, curly brown hair—it always reminded Casey of the curling ribbon she used on her Christmas gifts.

Casey headed for the loft at the end of the gym to get her books. It had been an extra-long workout. Chip was always willing to stay late, to give extra help when Casey or anyone else needed it. But once again she wondered if it would pay off. Would she make Elite the next spring and get a chance to be on the national team?

Casey ran up the steps to the loft that served as a study hall and lounging place for the team. *Not that we have much time for relaxation*, she thought. Now that it was the end of August, summer was almost over and she'd spent only a couple of days sailing on Lake Michigan.

She pulled a towel out of her gym bag and wiped the sweat off her face and neck, then shook out her damp, curly hair. Now that it was dark out, the window at the end of the loft reflected her silhouette. She sighed. At five feet one inch, she was a great height for gymnastics, but it was so hard to find clothes for school.

In the mirror Casey examined her face. She'd die if it broke out before school started next week. Bright blue eyes stared back at her. They were so blue, in fact, that people were always asking her if she wore colored contact lenses. She groaned as the light glinted off her braces. The orthodontist had told her that she had only a few more weeks left of them. But why couldn't they have come off before school started? Sometimes life just wasn't fair!

At the far end of the gym the light clicked off in Chip's office. She paused for a minute and looked down at her home away from home, the place where she spent a third of her life. Red, white, and blue murals of gymnasts in various poses decorated three of the pale blue walls, and large mirrors covered the fourth. A long ramp and an above-ground practice pit filled with foam ran along the wall opposite the loft.

Three sharp honks outside signaled her father's arrival.

"Bye, Casey!" Chip called out.

"See you tomorrow!" Casey answered as she ran down the stairs and out the club's main entrance. She opened the door to the family Honda, where her dad had been reading while he waited for her. Dropping her gym bag into the back, she sat down in the front seat and flipped the lever on the side of it. The bucket seat dropped into a reclining position. "Am I ever zonked!" she exclaimed.

Mr. Benson smiled at Casey. "Well, hello to you, too. Good workout, sugar?" He switched off the inside light and started the engine.

"Long workout," she answered, "but I finally got that new combination—once."

"That's my girl." A broad smile spread across his face. "How *is* everything at the gym?"

Casey stole a look at her dad. He maneuvered the car out of the parking lot and into the street.

Until five years ago, he had owned the Flyaway Gym Club, where he had started Casey in classes when she was four years old. "Bear" Benson was known throughout the gymnastic world for producing top-notch gymnasts, including several who had gained recognition on the National team. When she was nine, he had sold the club to Chip so he could go back to his first love—teaching. He had taken a job at Fairfield, the local high school, where he coached the girls' gymnastic team. But his interest in the club remained, and he always pumped Casey to tell him everything about the girls and the meets. "It's about the same," she told him.

"Will you have the new routine perfected by competition season?" he asked.

"I'm trying." Casey smiled. With her dad, no routine was ever ready until it was absolutely perfect. When she got to the high school, she'd have to work with him again. But for now she still had her ninth-grade year at Prescott. And that was going to be a blast.

"Practice, that's what it takes. Over and over— you know that."

"You and Chip even talk alike, Dad. That's all he ever says. Practice, practice—total dedication!"

Mr. Benson laughed as they came to a stop at a traffic light. "But seriously, Casey, he's a great coach. That's why I sold him the gym—and put your gymnastic career in his hands."

"I know, Dad." Casey closed her eyes and tried to relax her muscles.

"Oh, I almost forgot. Monica called and said you *absolutely had* to call her the instant you walked through the door." His green eyes twinkled as he mimicked her best friend's voice.

"Did she say anything else?"

He laughed again. "Just to call, but she sounded ready to burst."

Once they had parked in the driveway, Casey tore into the house and took the stairs two at a time to reach the phone in her bedroom. Dialing Monica's number, she wondered what her friend would have to say. Monica had left the gym only an hour before Casey had. But this was just like Monica. Something exciting had happened in the last hour, and she couldn't wait to share the news.

The phone rang twice before Monica picked it up.

"Hi, Monica, it's me. Sorry I'm so late." Casey flopped onto the rose-colored comforter on her bed.

"I thought you'd never call!" Monica squealed. "Chip must have really kept you."

"I wanted to get that new combination. I was desperate! Chip looked like he was ready to stay all night, too. Anyway, I finally did it. I just got home. What's up?"

"Well, you're not going to believe this, but on the way home, I saw *him*."

"Him? Who's that?" Casey couldn't imagine who Monica was talking about. She pictured her friend on the other end of the line. Monica always tucked her long, dark legs under her when she sat on her bed, almost as if she were working on her posture, with her back held perfectly straight. Monica's skin always reminded Casey of coffee with a little cream and her dark brown eyes were striking above her high cheekbones. She'd probably propped the phone in the crook of her neck so that she could brush her thick black hair. She brushed it constantly, to keep it looking neat.

"Bart, I saw Bart! Casey, where have you been? You know I've been drooling over him all summer." Monica sighed.

Casey remembered the tall basketball player from their junior high that her friend had been admiring. "So don't keep me in suspense! What happened?"

"I stopped to get milk for Mom and he was in the same line. Ohh, he's so gorgeous."

"That's all?"

"No. But I'll tell you the rest only if you come over and spend the night. Jo's already here. We don't have much time left till school starts, you know. We're going to plan our whole ninth grade tonight."

"Yeah, sure you are." Casey laughed and rolled over on her stomach. "You'll have to block off half of it for Flyaway."

"Come on, Casey! Hurry over. We're just hanging out here waiting for you," Jo urged her. She had obviously taken the phone from Monica.

"Okay, I will. Bye!" Casey hung up and headed downstairs. In the kitchen, her mom had already warmed up leftover dinner in the microwave. As Casey slid onto the bench in front of the table, she knocked down one of the baskets her mom had hung on the wall.

"Slow down, Casey!" Mrs. Benson laughed as she retrieved the fallen basket. She set a plate of steaming food in front of Casey. Her soft brown hair fell forward, and she brushed it back off her forehead. Her usual short, off-the-face style made her look taller than her five feet two inches. She handed Casey a glass of milk, and sat down across the table from her, as she did every night. "How's the back layout coming along?"

Casey nodded, her mouth full of broccoli.

"Good day at the gym?"

Casey swallowed. "Yeah, Chip stayed late to help me on the layout. But I finally got it." That was how the conversation started each evening. Mrs. Benson always wanted to know all the details, and she followed gymnastics as closely as her husband. Before Casey's older sister was born, her mom had been a physical education teacher, and she was a big sports fan.

"Great! I knew you could!" Mrs. Benson encouraged her.

"Did you get a letter from Barbara?" Casey asked. She missed her sister, who had left two weeks earlier for her freshman year at the University of Illinois.

Mrs. Benson shook her head. "Maybe tomorrow. But her tennis practices started this week, so who knows when we'll hear?"

Casey took a sip of milk. "Mom, can I spend the night at Monica's? Jo's going to be there, too." Casey thought about her two best friends. Both excellent gymnasts, exuberant Monica was such a contrast to Jo, whose quiet personality didn't quite hide her intense competitive nature.

"Go ahead." Mrs. Benson stood up and cleared Casey's plate. "I'm glad you have friends at the gym. It can get pretty lonely at the top if you don't."

As Casey raced back upstairs to get her stuff, she bumped into her older brother, who would be a senior at Fairfield High School that fall.

"Hi, Cheetah! How's the gym?" Tom asked. He stopped and grinned at her.

"Cut it out, Tom! You know I don't like that name!" In fact, Casey despised the nickname her brother and sister had given her when she was a little girl. They had always compared her to Tarzan's pet monkey. In spite of her ability to hang upside down on any available jungle gym and execute death drops on the playground bars, Casey had thought they were making fun of her short legs. However, her father had pointed out that she had the perfect body for a gymnast, and he had been right. But to Tom and Barbara, she was just a little monkey.

As he went downstairs, Tom let out a loud Tarzan yell—something he did when he wanted to torment her.

Oh, he thinks he's so cool, Casey said to herself, *the big football star at Fairfield.* She was glad he'd be graduated before she reached high school!

A half hour later, after a quick shower, Casey joined her friends at Monica's house. The bedroom occupied a prime corner of the stately two-story red-brick house located three streets from Casey's home. Monica had decorated the bedroom mostly in black and white, and there were big red throw pillows on the floor.

"I thought you'd never get here!" Monica said. "I've been telling Jo all about Bart." Monica sat down on her king-size bed, glowing with excitement.

"Did you actually *talk* to him?" Casey teased.

Monica tossed a red pillow at Casey. "No, silly— *he* talked to *me.* I was in line at Stater's. When I turned around he was standing right behind me."

"She almost fainted," Jo added, rolling her eyes.

"Well, I just stared at him—I couldn't talk at all," Monica continued. "Finally he said 'Hi!' and when I left, he said he'd see me at school next week."

"Fantastic! We're going to have so much fun being ninth graders." All summer Casey had looked forward to her last year at junior high.

Jo smiled. "Now we'll finally get our chance to be the big wheels."

Casey watched Jo, who sat painting her nails with pearly pink polish, her blond hair falling over one shoulder. She'd give anything to have Jo's gorgeous golden hair instead of her own thick, curly mop. And she loved Jo's eyes! One minute they were gray, the next turning gorgeous green. Jo was also fourteen, but somehow she seemed older. Maybe that came from taking care of her younger brothers and sisters, Casey thought.

"Yeah," Monica said in a dreamy voice. "Think of the boys."

Casey grimaced. "I'm not going to attract any boys with these horrible braces."

"Casey, you've got only a month to go." Jo waved her hands in the air to dry the nail polish.

"As a matter of fact, it's twenty-three days." Casey grinned. "Give or take a few hours."

"That's great! You'll be beautiful," Jo said, flashing her a phony movie-star smile. "But you know what? If we're on the Prescott gymnastics team, we're not going to have any time for boys. It'll be nonstop gymnastics."

Monica moaned. "Chip will work us out just as hard, even though we'll have to practice at Prescott, too."

"That's okay," Casey said. "We'll sweep the junior high league. Then Bart will *really* notice you."

"Besides, we've got Elite trials in the spring. That'll be so exciting!" Jo added.

"I know, I know." Monica sighed, rolled off the bed, and went to the window. "It'll be worse for me. I'm going to really have to strengthen my bars and beam if I want to make it."

"But your dance routines are dynamite!" Casey tried to sound encouraging, but she knew what Monica said was true. After changing from dancing to gymnastics, Monica had to struggle to keep up on some events. But Casey loved to watch her friend's floor exercise. She seemed to float in the air, and her tumbling runs were better than anyone else's at the club.

"You'll make it!" Jo jumped up and gave Monica a hug. "But we're all going to have to work hard."

By the time they piled into the king-size bed for the night, Casey felt excited about the upcoming year at Prescott. They hadn't planned everything, but there was one thing they did know: this year, Casey, Monica, and Jo would be the stars of the Prescott gymnastics team. Nothing would keep them from that.

Chapter 2

★ ★ ★ ★ ★ ★ ★ ★ ★ ★

THE next morning the girls straggled down to the kitchen at ten o'clock. A note from Monica's mother informed them that she had gone into her real estate office early that morning because she had an appointment to show a house. She'd left them a stack of Belgian waffles to microwave. For Casey it was a nice break from the healthful breakfasts Chip and Casey's parents insisted she eat every morning.

As they polished off the last of the waffles, topped with sliced peaches, the phone rang. Monica swallowed her last bite before she answered. "Hello? Oh, hi, Mom."

A frown deepened on Monica's face as she talked to her mother. Jo gave Casey a questioning look. What was up?

"What! Mom, they can't do that to us!" Monica looked as if she'd fallen off the beam in a championship meet. "Okay, I'll see you later." As she slowly hung up the phone, her friends stared at her.

Tears formed in Monica's eyes. "We can forget about our exciting year as super-cool ninth graders. They've changed the zoning. We have to go to Fairfield High."

Casey and Jo stared at Monica, who slumped into her chair. "You're kidding, right?" Jo asked.

Monica shook her head. "It's true. Mom read it in this morning's paper. The article said our whole neighborhood is going to Fairfield."

"How can they do that to us?" Jo looked as though she was about to start crying. "We'll be lowly freshmen."

Monica sighed. "Scrubs."

Casey put her head down on her arms and moaned. "My life is ruined! It's over!"

"So much for our year of being the top class." Jo tipped her chair back and then let it drop to the floor. The dishes on the glass-topped kitchen table rattled in response.

"At least we'll have gymnastics." Monica tried to smile. "Fairfield has a great team."

Casey moaned again. "You guys! I'll have to work with my dad. It was fun when I was a kid, but in high school?" She raised her head, thoroughly upset. "Tom will make my life miserable, I know that for a fact."

"Oh, Casey, I forgot. I'm sorry." Monica reached out and put her hand on Casey's arm. "But at least you'll make the team."

Jo's eyes widened. "We've *all* got to make it. I'll just die if I don't!"

"You'll make it," Casey assured Jo. "My dad knows how good you are."

Monica jumped up and started carrying the plates to the dishwasher. "And we'll show them that freshmen are better than the rest."

Casey shook her head. "Don't count on it. Dad's got a fantastic team."

"I know. And I'm going to be part of it!" Jo cried, standing up on her chair. "Bear Benson is the best high school coach in the state! Maybe even in the country. . . ."

Monica closed the dishwasher and turned to Casey. "He really is. Don't worry, Casey, you'll be okay. You get along great with your dad."

"I know." Casey nodded. "It's just such a shock. Here we thought we'd be stars at Prescott . . . and now we have to start all over at the high school."

"Look out, Fairfield! Here we come!" Jo said as she did a cheerleader jump off the chair.

Casey grinned at her friends. She wished she could share Jo's enthusiasm, but being at the same school as her father and her brother was definitely *not* going to be easy. At least she'd have Monica and Jo with her!

Later that morning Casey walked home. It was hard to believe the magical year they had looked forward to all summer had disappeared. Why did the city have to change the school district anyway, she mused. How could they move the boundary lines without considering how the kids would feel about it?

She stopped on the front sidewalk and took a look at her two-story red-brick house with its white trim. One of the shutters had not been hung straight after the latest paint job, and it gave the house a jaunty look. *If the city had its way, they'd probably move the houses around, too,* Casey thought.

The whole idea brought a smile to her face. They'd have trouble moving her house. It had been in the same place for many years, with the same family inside it. Casey knew it wouldn't give up without a fight.

As she pulled open the front door, she decided she would talk to her mom about going to Fairfield. Casey really missed having her sister around. Barbara was the person she usually talked to when she was upset or worried about something. *Why did Barbara have to go away to college? She could have gone to Northwestern and lived at home.*

In the kitchen Casey dropped her duffel bag onto the table. "Hi, Mom," she said glumly.

"What's wrong with you?" Mrs. Benson asked as she looked at Casey.

Casey sat down and leaned forward, resting her elbows on the table. "I have to go to Fairfield!"

"I heard. It was in this morning's paper."

"Mom, I can't go there!"

"I know you were excited about your last year at Prescott, but Fairfield isn't that bad. Barbara loved it, and Tom likes everything except the homework."

"That's the problem. Tom will be there," Casey explained.

Wiping her hands on a towel, her mom nodded and smiled. "Tom's teasing can be pretty bad. But he does it only in fun—because he likes to make you mad."

"Some fun," Casey muttered.

Mrs. Benson poured herself a cup of coffee. "Shall I make some hot chocolate for you?"

Casey put her head down on her arms. "No, I already had breakfast."

Trailing her hand across Casey's shoulders, Mrs. Benson sat down at the table. "I suspect that Tom isn't the only person at Fairfield you're worrying about."

Casey didn't answer right away. She wondered if her mom would understand how she felt. "Well . . . I will have dad for a coach," she said. "It'll be really weird."

Sighing, Mrs. Benson patted Casey's hand. "Will it be that terrible? You've worked with him before. You two were a great team."

Frustrated, Casey jumped up from her chair. "Mom, this is high school! You just don't understand how bad it's going to be! Nobody does!" She ran out of the kitchen.

After she went into her bedroom and slammed the door, Casey picked up her favorite teddy bear. Holding it closely to her, she pulled her photo album from seventh and eighth grades at Prescott out of the bookcase. She sat cross-legged on her bed and flipped through the book. Photographs of her with Monica and Jo covered the pages. She stopped at a picture of her favorite English teacher. Casey had been hoping to have her class again this year.

Why couldn't she have ninth grade at her old school? And how could she compete on a team where her dad was the coach? If she made the team, all the other girls would think it was only because she was Bear Benson's daughter.

And if she didn't make the team . . . it would be humiliating.

Casey tossed the photo album onto the floor and lay back on her bed. She closed her eyes and thought about her dad. How would *he* feel when he found out she'd be at Fairfield that fall?

At two o'clock Casey headed for the gym for her five-hour workout. It felt good to walk into the cool, air-conditioned club and escape the humid heat of another Chicago summer. During vacation Chip started practice earlier than usual so that the girls didn't have to stay so late. Still, practice cut into other activities like cookouts, days at the beach, and trips to the mall. But Casey didn't care. She'd rather be at Flyaway than anywhere else.

Monica and Jo were already working on the vault when she arrived. Chip motioned for her to join them.

The gym was humming with activity that afternoon. An assistant coach was working with a group of beginners learning kips to the uneven bars, and the Class II kids were at the beam. Casey stepped around a class of toddlers who were learning basic tumbling skills. A chubby four-year-old in a red leotard waved hello to Casey. The younger gymnasts idolized the older girls, just as Casey looked up to Mary Lou Retton. Casey smiled and waved back. She had started gymnastics at about the same age.

Casey ran up to the loft, took off her sweats, and hurried back downstairs to watch Jo's next vault. It was a handspring, full, the compulsory vault for Class I. Every girl would have to do the same vault on the first day of competition. Chip was determined to have the girls ready for the big meet next spring.

Jo bounced hard off the springboard and did a handspring onto the horse. Then she did a full twist off the vault. Her flight through the air was high and she landed perfectly—with no steps at all.

"That's the best you've done so far." Chip grinned and gave Jo a thumbs-up sign.

Casey saw Jo smile at his compliment. Chip was so generous with his praise when a gymnast was performing well. She swallowed a giggle. *That's the only way to keep us working so hard,* she thought.

Monica smiled as Casey walked over and joined her. "I can't believe they have to change the routines now. I just got the old ones down!"

"Every four years." Casey laughed at Monica's reaction to the changes that occurred after each Olympics. As girls learned to perform more difficult tricks at younger and younger ages, the compulsories were changed to ensure competition at a high level of skill. But since Monica was still fairly new to gymnastics, she found it hard to adjust to the changes.

"It's like starting all over," Monica complained. She moved into place and waited while Chip pulled the springboard back for her. Because she was taller, she needed extra distance from the vault to complete her twist.

"Stretch, Monica!" Chip yelled. "Use that extra height!"

Although her vault was lower than Jo's, Monica landed solidly, with only a couple of hops on the mat. Chip gave her a playful poke as she started back down the runway. "It's getting better—keep it up." Then he quickly readjusted the springboard. "Okay, Casey. Let's nail it!"

Casey sprinted down the runway, gaining speed before she hit the board, and sailed into her first twist. Twisting off the back of the vault, she landed nicely and then sat down on the mat.

Jo and Monica laughed as Casey jumped to her feet.

"Well, that was a surprise ending," Chip observed, smiling. "Planning on using that at the Elite trials?"

"No, I just thought I'd rest for a while, after that *superb* vault."

Chip chuckled. "Get out of here!"

"You're kicking me out? You mean I'm free for the whole afternoon?" Casey teased.

"I'll kick you, all right." Chip laughed.

Casey ran back to the other girls. "Yes, sir."

Chip shook his head, chuckling. "Okay. I want all of you to do ten more!"

After vault, Casey's enthusiasm disappeared as she began to worry about making the high school team. She just couldn't seem to keep her mind on the workout, and her routines showed it. She missed her hands on a simple catch to the high bar and fell off the beam more than she stayed on. At the end of the workout, when everyone was getting ready to leave, Chip asked Casey to stay for a few minutes.

Chip motioned her into his office in the front corner of the gym and closed the door. "Have a seat, Casey. I'm just wondering if something's bothering you. You weren't acting like yourself out there today—especially not on the beam. What's wrong?" he asked, sitting behind his desk.

Casey stared at the floor. "It's nothing."

"Hey! Don't forget, I've known you for a long time. I can tell when there's a problem," Chip said.

"Okay, okay. They've changed the zoning and I have to go to Fairfield this year," Casey told him, dropping into a chair.

"I see. So now your dad will be coaching you again."

"It wasn't so bad when I was little, but now I'm afraid it's going to be awful."

Pushing back his Cubs baseball cap, Chip ran his hand through his sun-streaked hair. "Look at it this

way. Fairfield is a great team." He leaned over and
punched her arm. "And you'll get rid of me for the
high school season!"

Casey gave him a weak smile. "I don't want to
get rid of you. Besides, all the older girls will think
Dad put me on the team just because I'm his
daughter."

"Casey, come on. You'll have no trouble making
the team on your own. You don't need anyone's
help. They'll be able to see that. And remember—
your dad's one of the best coaches in the state."

"But he still is my dad," she reminded Chip. "At
least I won't get him as a teacher right away." Mr.
Benson taught physiology for juniors and seniors
at Fairfield.

Chip swiveled back and forth in his chair. "I had
the same thing happen to me when I was a kid,
you know."

"You were a kid once?"

"Hey! That's more like the Casey I know." He
grinned. "When I was in Boy Scouts, my father was
the scoutmaster. He made me work so hard, I practically had to pass my Tenderfoot badge twice."

Casey laughed. Talking to Chip always made her
feel better. She'd miss practice at Flyaway while
she competed at Fairfield during the high school
season.

As if reading her mind, Chip added, "Bear asked
me to assist at some of the meets, so you won't be
completely free of me."

"That's great," Casey said. "I'm glad."

"Good. Now, when you get to the first workout,
give 'em all you've got. You're as talented as any
girl there. In fact, Jo could be your biggest competition."

Casey thanked Chip and left his office in better

spirits. Maybe her freshman year would turn out okay. She'd have to give the high school team a chance.

Late that night Casey stood in her dark bedroom, looking out the large window at the yard below. She knew she wouldn't be able to sleep at all. She was excited about the first day of school tomorrow, yet she was scared at the same time. It would be so different from going back to Prescott, where she knew everyone and was already guaranteed a spot on the team.

She glanced at the clock. It was quarter to eleven. She hoped it wasn't too late to make a phone call.

She reached for the phone and dialed Jo's number. Luckily, Jo answered. "Hi, Jo!" Casey said as cheerfully as she could.

"Oh, Casey, I'm *so* glad you called. I'm in the kitchen making some hot chocolate. I'm so nervous, I can't sleep," Jo complained.

"Me either," Casey said as she sat down on her bed and leaned against the headboard. "I wonder if we'll ever fit in there."

"At least we'll be on the team. We will make it, won't we, Casey?"

"I think so. They don't have too many kids from private clubs like we are. But we'll still have to prove ourselves. Dad will make us earn our spot." *Boy, will he,* Casey thought to herself. She knew how tough he was on the Fairfield team, having seen a few practices of his.

"But we're only freshmen," Jo said. "We'll have to start all over in everything. No one will even know who we are."

"But, Jo, a year from now everyone will—after

we make the team and win the state championships." The more Casey assured Jo, the better she
felt about the whole thing herself. "I'll meet you at
the corner in the morning, okay?"

"Okay. Bye, Casey. Hope you get some sleep."

Casey hung up the phone and climbed under the
covers. *Maybe Fairfield won't be so bad after all,*
she thought to herself. *Or maybe I'm just dreaming!*

Chapter 3

★ ★ ★ ★ ★ ★ ★ ★ ★ ★

As Casey, Jo, and Monica reached the front of the large red-brick school, they stopped a minute to look at the busy scene. Students were milling around on all sides of the building, and dozens more were getting out of school buses that had just arrived.

"Ooh, it's so exciting," Monica said, clutching her spiral-bound notebooks to her chest.

"Not to mention scary," Casey added.

Jo grabbed Casey's arm. "Come on, Case, we're going to have a great year!"

Casey had to smile. Jo's natural optimism was catching.

On their way into the building the three girls cut across a corner of the front yard where the seniors were performing the yearly ritual of sitting in beach chairs and watching all the underclassmen go by. A chorus of yells surprised Casey.

"Hey, you're not a senior!" A tall boy stood up and walked toward Casey.

Startled, the three girls quickly leapt off the grass back onto the sidewalk.

"Apparently, one does *not* disturb the seniors," Monica said in a haughty tone. Jo giggled.

23

"What a great way to start the school year," Casey remarked.

Once inside, the girls got separated because they had to go to different lines to pick up their locker assignments. After Casey found her locker and put her jacket inside, she headed to the corner where she had planned to meet Monica and Jo—only she couldn't find it, at first. Fairfield was such a big school, and there were so many corners! Finally, after wandering up and down three very long halls, Casey found her friends and began to feel better about her first day. It might take her a while, but she would find her way around on her own.

But just as she had thought she was getting it all together, she saw her brother, Tom, approaching with a few fans trailing behind him.

"Groupies!" Casey scoffed to her friends. "Just because he scored the most touchdowns last year, he's supposed to be this hero." Actually, she didn't know how good he was; she hadn't had time to go to any of his football games, since she was always at the gym.

Spotting Casey, Tom waved and let out one of his infamous Tarzan yells. "Hi, Cheetah!" he yelled.

Mortified, Casey turned and ran down a side hall. How could he do that to her? Why did she have to come to this school? She fled into the bathroom and put her notebook down on the counter. She went to the sink and splashed her face with cold water to calm down.

"Why'd you take off like that?" Monica asked, walking in with Jo. "That's just what he wanted."

Jo handed Casey some paper towels to dry her face.

"I hate it when he does that. But *he* seems to think it's funny," Casey said.

Monica shifted the books in her arms. "You'll just have to ignore him," she said.

"How can I ignore loud Tarzan yells that echo in the halls? He'll pester me all year."

Jo handed Casey her notebook. "We'll get him back somehow. C'mon, we've got to find our first class before we're late."

By lunch hour Casey felt much better. Her teachers seemed fairly nice, and so far no one had mentioned the fact that she was Bear Benson's daughter or Tom Benson's sister.

In the cafeteria she looked for Monica and Jo as she pushed her tray through the food line. Taking a hamburger and a small paper cup of unidentifiable dessert, she scanned the mob of students for a familiar face. The place was jammed. How would she ever find them?

Along one side of the room a group of older girls had pushed two tables together, and they were eating lunches they had brought from home. As Casey walked toward them, one girl looked up at her and nudged the girl next to her. She leaned over and whispered something, and then both girls smiled at Casey.

Is something wrong with me—other than being a freshman? Casey thought. She gripped her lunch tray more tightly and continued to hunt for her friends. As she went by the large table, one of the girls said, "Hi! Need a place to sit? We've got some room," she offered cheerfully.

"M-me?" Casey stammered. Why were they asking her to eat with them? They looked like seniors.

The brown-haired girl moved over to make room for Casey. "I'm Sara. Aren't you Tom Benson's little sister?"

So that's it, Casey thought. They thought they could get to Tom by being nice to her. She wondered how often that would happen in the coming year. "Yes, I am," she told Sara. "But no thanks, I'm looking for some friends. I promised I'd sit with them."

"Some other time then." Sara smiled and turned back to her group.

As Casey moved away, she saw Jo waving at her from the far corner of the cafeteria. She threaded her way between the crowded tables and collapsed in the chair they'd saved for her.

"Where have you been?" Jo demanded.

"I've been turning down invitations to lunch at the senior girls' table," Casey said. She took a small bite of hamburger, which looked suspiciously like the ones they'd had at Prescott—dry and horrible.

"What!" Monica almost dropped her milk carton. "They asked you to eat with them?"

Jo stared at Casey. "I don't believe it."

"Well, believe it. But it's only because I'm Tom's sister." Casey gave up on the burger and poked at the strange dessert on her tray. "What's this?"

Monica shrugged. "Who knows? So they think they'll be your friend and then get close to Tom?"

"That's a laugh." Casey grinned. "Tom and I don't talk much at all. I wouldn't even *want* to get close to him."

Jo sat up straighter to see where the seniors were sitting. "Look at it this way, Monica. We could be known as Tom's sister's friends."

"Instant popularity," Monica added.

"Forget it." Casey finished the mysterious dessert—she was pretty sure it was some sort of pudding—and pushed her tray away. "Monica, have you seen Bart yet?"

Monica sighed. "I found out his area didn't get rezoned. He's still at Prescott."

"Too bad! Maybe he'll call you," Jo said.

"Now that we're here . . . I don't know. Somehow it won't be the same." Monica looked around the crowded cafeteria. "On to someone new."

Casey laughed. "I think you'll be able to find someone here . . . or maybe twenty someones."

Lunchtime ended much too quickly, in Casey's opinion. She wasn't sure if she was ready to face her last two classes. As she waited to dump the trash from her tray, a slim, blond-haired girl bumped into her.

"Oh, sorry. How's it going?" she asked politely.

"Okay." Casey studied the pretty girl who smiled at her, and admired the baby's breath tucked into her thick French braid. She looked slightly familiar. Casey wondered if she was on her dad's team.

"My name's Jill Ramsey."

"Hi." Casey couldn't help but wonder why this person was being so nice to her.

Jill smiled, revealing a dimple in her cheek. "You look a lot like Tom Benson. Are you related, by any chance?"

Casey dumped her tray and turned to go. Tom again! But she couldn't be rude; after all, Jill was being nice to her. "I'm his sister," she answered. "Casey."

"I hope you have a good year!" Jill called after her as she left the cafeteria.

"Thanks," Casey muttered. If she didn't know better, she'd swear Jill's friendly smile was for real. It looked like the only people she was going to meet at Fairfield wanted to meet her brother, the football star. *Well, it was better than nothing,* Casey figured.

Chapter 4

★ ★ ★ ★ ★ ★ ★ ★ ★ ★

CASEY hurried to the locker room after journalism, which had turned out to be her favorite class so far. She whirled the combination on her gym locker and quickly started changing for the first gymnastics practice before tryouts.

Suddenly, she stopped. This was it—the day she'd have to prove herself. Now she would have to work with her dad and fight for a spot on the team. A dozen butterflies started playing a soccer game in her stomach.

The crowded locker room buzzed with girls calling back and forth to each other. *There must be thirty kids in here,* Casey thought, *all wanting a place on the team.* The competition would be fierce.

Jo raced in and threw her books down on the bench beside Casey. "I'm so excited!" she said.

Casey took a deep breath and tried to steady her nerves. "Me, too. Where's Monica?"

"She's trying to talk her way out of detention from Mrs. Laird. Too much socializing in science lab."

"I hope she makes it. Dad's an absolute fanatic

about being on time." Casey pulled on the plain blue leotard she had chosen to wear. Today she wanted to blend into the crowd and hide the fact she might get special attention because she was Bear's daughter.

"Okay, Casey. Let's go show them what we can do!" Jo said, slamming her locker shut.

Casey smiled as she followed her friend toward the gym. Jo was so competitive. Casey wondered what would happen if Jo didn't make the team. *It would only ruin her whole life,* she thought.

As they started into the gym, they heard Monica's voice behind them. "I'm here! I talked her out of it!" she yelled.

"Just hurry!" Casey called over her shoulder as she and Jo left the locker room.

The gym occupied part of a large building with basketball courts on the other side of a sliding wall. The walls were decorated by two bands of royal blue and gold, the school colors, painted around the top, near the ceiling. A large mural of an Aztec waving a tomahawk covered one end wall.

Casey and Jo joined the group of prospective gymnasts on the bleachers, saving some space for Monica. Most of the girls clustered in small groups as they came in from the locker room. Casey could feel the excitement in the air.

Suddenly, Casey heard a girl behind her whisper, "There's the Benson kid. You can bet *she'll* make the team."

Casey felt her chest tighten. This was exactly what she'd been afraid of. Making herself breathe deeply, she shook out her hands to release the tension in her body.

Jo reached over and put her hand on Casey's

arm. "It'll be okay," she whispered. "Do you know *anybody*?"

"Not really." Casey shook her head. "The two back there are in my algebra class. And there's that girl I met in the cafeteria." Casey watched as Jill Ramsey walked into the gym.

When she saw Casey, Jill flashed her a big smile. "We meet again!" she said as she climbed up the bleachers past Casey to join her friends.

Monica scampered in and sat between them just as Coach Benson emerged from his office at the end of the gym. "I made it!" she whispered.

"Just barely," Jo commented, moving over a little.

Casey watched her dad cross the gym floor in long strides. His casual tan pants and yellow and white rugby shirt made him look younger than his forty-two years. He greeted the girls in front and nodded at Casey. "I'm glad to see we have a good turnout. That'll give us a chance to pick the very best team."

Monica squeezed Casey's arm. "I hope that means us," she said in a soft voice.

Casey smiled and turned back to her dad, who was introducing his assistant coaches and explaining the procedure for choosing the final team.

"In the end we'll have to pick only twelve of you. As I look around, I see that may be difficult to do this year. Perhaps we'll have to have some alternates." Bear ran a hand through his short, curly hair generously laced with gray. "But then, I know how hard it is being an alternate."

Whispers started among the girls, and Casey suspected they were discussing her dad's background. He had once been an alternate at the Pan American Games, and although it had been a great honor, he had hated not competing.

"Today we'll take a look at what level you're at and give you a chance to show us your stuff," Bear continued. "Then we'll put you in groups according to ability. Tryouts will be held in two weeks."

Bear then divided the girls into four groups, one for each event. Casey, Jo, and Monica were all at a different apparatus. Casey noticed that her father had assigned them to their specialties. Monica was on floor exercise, Jo had been assigned the bars, and she would start out on the balance beam. This way they would have a better chance to prove themselves to the older girls. Score one for her dad!

Casey hung back and let the other girls in her group go first. It was obvious that some hadn't had much training, but Casey admired them for trying. It took a lot of courage.

The young assistant coach motioned to Casey. "Go ahead. It's your turn."

Casey wondered if he knew who she was. Maybe her dad had warned the other coaches to treat her just like everyone else. She certainly hoped so.

Pressing up to a handstand, Casey mounted the beam and went through a compulsory Class I routine. It wasn't difficult, and she was glad she knew it backward and forward.

Casey completed her front handspring and danced down the beam as if it were a large plank instead of only four inches wide. She floated effortlessly through her routine, thrilling to the sense of freedom as she soared above the beam in a double stag leap. When she completed her dismount without having to take a step, Casey saw several people had been watching her.

One of the girls from her algebra class came up to Casey. "That was great!" she said. "I wish I could do that."

"Just keep working on it and you'll get it," Casey told her. *I'm starting to sound like Dad!* she thought to herself. But Casey felt sorry for all the beginners. From what she had seen so far, they didn't have a chance of making the Fairfield team.

Throughout the workout, Casey, Monica, and Jo stayed in their separate groups. They didn't get an opportunity to talk until they met in the locker room at seven-thirty.

"What did you think?" Monica asked as she stuffed her leotard into her gym bag.

"It was terrific!" Jo jumped on the bench and did a little dance step down its length, as if she were on the beam. "I just know we're going to make it." She hopped down and leaned against a locker. "Wasn't it just the greatest, Casey?"

A grin stole across Casey's face. "I loved it! At least, once I started breathing." She leaned down to tie her sneakers. "I was so scared Dad would introduce me as his daughter, or make some other dumb comment."

"You've been worrying for nothing," Jo assured her.

Frowning, Casey pulled on her sweatshirt. "We *are* freshmen. I wonder if that will make a difference."

"We'll just have to prove that we're the best." Monica struck a victory pose. "Show them that age doesn't count."

Casey smiled. She thought they were all good enough to make the team, but there were only twelve spots, after all. "I hope you're right," she said.

* * *

For a week workouts stressed developing necessary skills. Several of the girls dropped out after the first few days, but the easy pace set by the coaches trying to teach the routines frustrated Casey. She wanted to work on her new beam combination, but she didn't want anyone to think she was showing off. So instead she went over and over her compulsories, trying to add more of her own style to them.

When Bear finally announced that the tryouts would be held the next Monday, Casey, Monica, and Jo were actually relieved.

"I'll be so glad to get it over with," Casey said as the girls walked home together after practice Friday night.

"Me, too!" Jo exclaimed. "This waiting is killing me!"

Monica sighed. "I don't know. I just hope I make it."

"Oh, Monica, you'll make it." Jo shifted her books to her other arm.

"I don't know, some of those girls are really good."

Casey felt anxious, too, but she wasn't about to admit it. If she acted confident, she knew it would help her to feel that way, too. "Yeah, they *are* good. But we're better!" she said enthusiastically. She just had to hope that she would be in top form on Monday.

The weekend dragged by, but finally it was Monday afternoon and the tryouts were about to begin. Casey sat on the bleachers, twisting her hands. She couldn't remember feeling so nervous since her first Class I meet. Jo joined her, and together they watched Monica finish up her final warmups on floor exercise.

"She's great, isn't she?" Casey said, leaning back on her elbows.

Jo watched intently as Monica finished exactly with the music. "I wish I could nail floor exercise like that."

"Don't be greedy. You're the ace on bars." Casey laughed, poking Jo. "Besides, remember all those years of dancing Monica took."

Jo clenched her teeth, her lips pressed into a firm line. "I know, but I've got to place in everything."

"Ease up, Jo, these are only tryouts," Casey told her.

"But I still want to win," Jo said.

Monica wiped her face with a small towel and looked around. She waved at her friends. They were trying out in their original groups, so the three friends wouldn't be together.

Casey looked up as Chip came in the side door. "Hey, there's Chip! I'm going to go talk to him."

Jo was busy concentrating on the final warmups, trying to size up the competition. "I'll be over," she mumbled as she stared at another girl's bar routine.

As Casey climbed down the bleachers and walked over to Chip, her dad came up on the other side of him.

"Good to see you! Want to help judge?" Bear asked. He shook Chip's hand vigorously.

"No, thanks!" Chip draped his arm around Casey's shoulder as she came up to him. "I'm a little biased. I just came to provide moral support." He turned to Casey. "Need any?"

"Tons!" Casey laughed.

Mr. Benson ignored Casey's comment. "Well, in that case," he said to Chip, "you'd better find a seat in the bleachers. We're almost ready to start."

The girls had been told earlier that the tryouts would consist of four routines, plus some extra work on the mat to show their tumbling skills.

Bear announced he would judge all the vaults first, then the girls would split into their groups. "As in a regular competition, each of you will have two chances to do your vault," he said.

As everyone sat down on one side of the runway, Casey noticed that the original number of competitors had dwindled. She counted only twenty-two girls left.

Bear stood by the horse, changing the springboard for each girl, giving each one her score. After the first vault he offered tips to improve their second attempt.

Casey sprinted down the runway and executed a high vault. After she landed, she paused, waiting to hear Bear's suggestions for her next vault. But he only nodded for her to continue.

What does that mean? she wondered. She completed her second vault, then sat back down next to Jo. "How did I look?" she asked.

"Great, as usual." Jo linked her arm through Casey's and whispered, "We're going to do it!"

After her floor exercise Casey leaned against the bleachers on one side of the gym. From where she was standing, she could see all the other groups performing. Nervous tension still knotted her stomach, but she was pretty sure she could hold her own against the rest. Now, if only her dad wanted her on the team.

She watched Jill Ramsey as the senior gracefully worked through the uneven parallel bars. Her long blond hair, again French braided, accented her high cheekbones and delicate features. As Casey watched the smooth routine, she knew Jill would be on the team for her third year.

Jill had been so nice to her during the last two weeks that Casey had to wonder again if she just wanted to meet Tom, like all the others. The only senior girls who hadn't fallen all over her were the ones trying out for the team, and they seemed to dislike her. She wondered how she would have felt if someone else were the coach's daughter.

A soft gasp of "Oh, no!" caught Casey's attention, and she turned to see Monica climbing back on the beam. Casey closed her eyes and sighed. Monica never should have fallen on her compulsory routine. She usually had trouble with her optional skills, but not this one. Casey desperately hoped that losing half a point wouldn't keep her friend off the team.

Monica resumed the routine where she had left off, and finished with a solid dismount. She smiled at Bear, then searched for Casey. When she found her, she walked over and announced, "Well, I just blew it!"

"Put it out of your mind," Casey reassured Monica. "You have only floor left, and that's your best event."

"Easy for you to say." Monica forced a smile. "But I'll try."

Monica returned to her group, and Casey moved to the bars. She volunteered to go first so she could watch Monica's best and last event.

Since floor exercise and beam always took longer than the bars and vault, others gathered in front of the spring floor to watch. The taped music was the same for everyone, but each girl added her own style and skills to the routine. Casey's own strength was in the three tumbling runs spaced throughout the three minutes.

Monica stood posed in the corner of the forty-square-foot floor. As the music started, she began to dance through her routine. Her years of studying ballet were evident as Monica interpreted the music beautifully.

As Monica reached the last tumbling run, Casey held her breath. But Monica completed the back aerial somersault with a full twist with ease. She spun to a final pose as the music ended, and almost everyone in the gym began to applaud.

Casey watched her dad's expression. She knew Monica had come through, and that the fall from the beam would be forgotten. At least one of them would make the team.

After tryouts the girls gathered in the locker room.

"I wish I could go to bed and sleep for days." Jo leaned against her locker and closed her eyes. "You could wake me when they announce the team."

"Don't we wish." Monica laughed. "Does anybody know when we find out?"

Casey shook her head. "He didn't say. But it will seem like forever."

But just before they all left the gym, Bear opened the door to the locker room and announced that he would post the list of his team selections the next day at noon.

That night dinner at the Bensons seemed to last a lifetime. Casey studied her father carefully for any sign that she'd made the team, but he cleverly steered the conversation away from gymnastics.

Instead, he and Tom discussed Fairfield High's chances for a winning football season, while Casey nervously waited to see if he would say anything.

Casey helped her mom clear the plates and serving bowls and then sat down at the table.

Mrs. Benson opened the oven and pulled out a pan of apple crisp. She served some into a bowl and set it in front of Casey.

"Oh, Mom," Casey said. "Dessert! And it's my favorite!" In spite of her nervous stomach, she started in on the sweet treat. Desserts were rare in their house, and Casey wondered what the special occasion was. She smiled to herself. Maybe they were preparing her for the ax tomorrow, like giving a prisoner one last delicious meal before the execution.

"Two little boys came to the door with a wagonload of apples and I couldn't turn them down," Mrs. Benson said as everyone complimented her on the dessert.

Mr. Benson pushed his chair away from the table and stood up. He leaned over and ruffled Casey's hair. "How's school, sugar? Mrs. Sullivan said you were a great English student."

"It's fine, Dad," Casey answered. She hoped she was also a great gymnast!

He picked up his coffee mug. "I'll take this with me, if you don't mind. I have some work to do, so I'll be in the study."

He's going to work on the list, Casey thought as she watched him leave the room. Reluctantly, she turned away to help with the dishes. She dropped a handful of silverware trying to get it into the basket in the dishwasher, and then almost dropped a ceramic bowl she was washing.

"I'll do this tonight." Mrs. Benson took the plates

out of Casey's hands. "Or else we won't have anything to eat on tomorrow!" she joked.

Casey was glad to escape from the kitchen. She went to the study, but the door was closed. She tiptoed past, but she couldn't hear anything except her dad's squeaky desk chair. She wondered who he had already put down on the list . . . she *had* to be on it, she just had to!

Chapter 5

★ ★ ★ ★ ★ ★ ★ ★ ★ ★

BEFORE lunch on Tuesday Casey raced to the bulletin board outside the girls' locker room. She wanted to be the first to see who had made the team.

There it was! The list had been posted. She took a deep breath and ran her finger down the alphabetical list. When she'd passed the B's, she stopped, slumping against the wall, a knot starting to form in her stomach.

She wasn't on the list.

Suddenly, she remembered Monica and Jo. Gathering her courage, she went back to the list. She found both names. Casey stood staring into space. Relief that her friends had made it was followed by disappointment that slowly turned into anger. It wasn't fair! *How could he leave me off?* she thought. *I was as good as anyone else!*

Who else did he choose? As she read through the rest of the list, a smile came over her face. The seniors had been listed first. She had found Monica and Jo with the other underclassmen—and her name was there, too! She had made the team!

Now all she had to do was to show her dad and

the rest of the team that they could count on her. She couldn't wait!

That afternoon during sixth period the public address system crackled for attention and Bear Benson's voice came over the loudspeaker.

"This is a reminder that all members of the girls' gymnastics team should report to the gym after school for an organizational meeting. This is mandatory!"

Casey looked up from the pile of yearbooks she was studying in her journalism class. *Well, here we go,* she thought. This was the beginning—the first meeting for the team. And she was part of it! A shiver tickled her spine, and she spent the rest of the period trying not to watch the clock every second.

Finally, class ended and she hurried to the gym. She found a place to sit next to Monica and Jo.

Jo leaned over and whispered, "We're the only freshmen—no sophomores, either. I hope the others don't bug us about that."

Casey nodded. "Yeah, it'll be bad enough having Dad as the coach."

The older juniors and seniors talked and called to one another as each new group came into the room. No one said anything to the three freshmen.

"Looks like we're being ignored," Monica observed. She leaned back on the bleacher behind her.

Casey shrugged. She was starting to get used to it. After being the oldest gymnasts at the Flyaway Gym Club, being on the low end of the totem pole was going to be difficult. "Remember—we bumped some of their buddies off the team," she reminded her friend.

"Did they lose only five seniors last year?" Jo asked.

Nodding, Casey watched the senior girls talking together. She knew a few of them belonged to Tom's crowd. One dark-haired girl had gone to the Christmas formal with Tom the year before.

Jill Ramsey came through the gym door, and everyone turned to greet her.

Jo poked Casey in the arm. "Who's she?"

"Looks like she's top banana here," Monica added.

The slim gymnast spoke to each girl as she came in. When she saw Casey, she gave her a big smile. "Hi! Glad you made the team!" she said. Then she sat in front with a redhead whom Casey knew from hearing her father talk about her the year before. Her name was Ginny and she was a great vaulter.

Monica raised an eyebrow and looked at Casey suspiciously. "How do you know her?" she asked.

"I met her in the cafeteria. I guess she knows Tom," Casey answered.

"At least *you* have an in. Maybe these other girls will talk to you sometime this year," Jo said.

"Hey!" Monica sat up quickly. "Here comes your dad."

Bear came out, and the group quickly became silent. He greeted the gymnasts and, as before, only nodded curtly at Casey and her friends. "Okay, girls. You all know what we're here for."

"A winning season!" Ginny volunteered.

"Right, Ginny. And what does that take?"

"Work! Work! Work!" one girl called out.

"Total dedication! Physical training! Handling stress without crumbling. It's all a part!" Bear Benson emphasized each statement with a raised fist.

"You forgot fun!" someone interjected.

Bear laughed and adjusted the whistle he wore around his neck. "That, too—occasionally."

The girls cheered, and Casey noticed most of them were smiling. She was glad they liked her dad. He *was* a great coach.

Continuing his pep talk, Casey's father became even more excited. "We can do it! We can win the league again!"

A girl in the back muttered, "It's the same speech every year." Someone giggled.

Casey rolled her eyes. "Yeah, but I have to *live with it*," she quipped. But Jo and Monica didn't hear her—they, too, were caught up in Bear's enthusiasm. She sighed. *If I'm going to be part of this, I guess I better try to forget he's my dad and join in,* she told herself.

"Practice starts tomorrow," Bear announced.

"So soon!" several voices called in surprise.

Bear grinned. "Hey! We *could* start today."

"No, tomorrow's perfect!" Ginny quickly answered.

"It'll give us a chance to warm up, and then we'll really hit it next week," Bear continued. "If you haven't already switched into sixth period gym, do that right away. We'll begin workout every day at one-forty."

"Oh, no! I forgot about that." Casey grabbed Jo's arm. "Now I have to switch out of my journalism class."

Monica leaned over to get in on the conversation. "Can't you take it another time?"

"I hope so." Casey hated the thought of losing her favorite class. She'd looked forward to working on the school yearbook—and she had hoped that for once, another hobby wouldn't interfere with gymnastics.

"Girls, listen up! No talking!" Bear frowned at Casey, and she heard a giggle behind her. Casey gulped. He had made it obvious she wasn't going to get away with anything just because she was the coach's daughter. She guessed their relationship would be different at school than it was at home.

Before he dismissed them, Mr. Benson announced that he had ordered tapes of the 1988 Olympic finals. "I couldn't get a definite date, but when they come, we'll show them in slow motion and take a good look."

"Are these the same as we saw on TV?" Jill asked.

Bear seemed glad that someone was paying attention to him. "No, these are special. We'll see each and every top gymnast's routines, and they're all filmed with a closeup lens."

As the girls left the gym a few minutes later, Casey heard several comments about the videos. Everyone seemed excited about seeing them, and about the prospects for a winning season.

This might be the best team Dad's ever coached, Casey thought to herself. *And I'm on it!*

Wednesday morning Casey came out of her counselor's office and found Monica and Jo waiting for her. "They don't *have* another journalism class!" she blurted out angrily. "And everything else that's decent is full."

"Uh-oh." Monica grimaced and caught a book that threatened to topple off the pile in her arms. "What did you get?"

"You won't believe this, but I have to take *art.*"

"Art!" Monica shrieked. Two boys at nearby lockers looked over at them.

Jo started laughing. "Last year you painted the worst poster in the whole class."

"I know." Casey sighed. "How'd you guys do?"

"They have English every hour, so it was no big deal for me," Jo said.

"Me either," Monica added. "Are you going to art today?"

Casey nodded. "Yeah . . . oh, I can't *believe* I'm taking art!"

"Don't worry," Jo consoled her. "I'll walk you to class. I go in that direction."

Casey pretended to pout. "Okay, but you've got to promise to hold my hand," she joked.

At their lockers they dumped off most of their books, and then Casey and Jo hurried toward the far end of one wing of the school, where the art classrooms were located.

Casey was practically out of breath when she arrived. After saying good-bye to Jo she paused at the door and watched the activity taking place inside. Some students were getting out supplies, and some had already started working. It looked like everyone had their own special project. *Maybe the teacher will let me do a finger-painting project,* Casey thought to herself, smiling.

She walked in and handed her transfer card to the art teacher, Mr. Green. She had almost expected him to be wearing a smock and a funny hat like she'd seen in pictures. Instead, he wore a blue polo shirt and had a gold chain around his neck. He looked more like a baseball coach.

"How much art have you had, Casey?" he asked.

"Almost none," she admitted. "I had to change because of the gymnastics team and this is all that was open."

"Are you trying to tell me this wasn't your number-one choice?" Mr. Green tried to look stern, but his eyes gave him away. Casey sighed with relief when she saw he was teasing her.

"I just never thought of it." She looked around the crowded room for a familiar face, but she didn't recognize anyone.

"You can sit over there." Mr. Green pointed to an empty chair at a table where a boy stood in front of a mound of red clay. "Brett! Come over and meet your new partner."

The blond boy looked up from his work, then started over. He was about medium height, and Casey noticed muscles under his surfer-style T-shirt. His hair was almost as curly as hers, and a wide smile lit up his face. He was gorgeous! Casey smiled back, hoping her braces weren't too noticeable.

"Hi! I'm Brett Kelly!" He extended his hand and flashed her another big smile. Looking into his blue-gray eyes, Casey started to shake his hand. At the last second she glanced down to see his hand covered with thick red clay.

"Agh!" She jumped back as he started to laugh.

Mr. Green cleared his throat. "Very funny. Brett, please show Casey what goes on in here. Then start her working on some clay. I'll check on you later." He nodded and went back to his desk to finish taking attendance.

Brett waved his gooey red hand in Casey's face and grinned. "I *almost* fooled you."

Casey wasn't sure how to react, so she laughed. "I hope you don't mind helping me."

"You certainly are short!"

"I'm not *that* short," Casey argued. She stood as straight as she could, trying to look taller than her five feet one inch. What if he hated short girls?

"Anyway, I'm a gymnast. They're supposed to be short," she told Brett.

"Oh, no! I'm not complaining. I like standing next to you—you make me look like a basketball player." He grinned again.

Brett got another chunk of clay from a large pail and demonstrated how to knead it and cut through it with a wire to get rid of the air bubbles. Then he shoved the clay toward her. "Okay, Michelangelo, get to work."

For the rest of the period Casey divided her time between trying to control the large lump of clay and watching Brett's fantastic profile. She would definitely like to get to know him better, and wondered if there was any chance they could be more than desk partners.

After art class the day dragged by. Casey could hardly wait to get to practice. Even working with her dad didn't seem so bad, since no one—including Bear—had made a big thing about her being his daughter.

Excited once she was in the gym, Casey stood looking at the gymnastics equipment set out in four areas. Just being in the gym set Casey's pulse racing, and she pictured herself helping to win the League championship. . . . A gym full of Fairfield students would be cheering in the background as she finished her routine . . . then a ten would flash on the score card, and as the applause became deafening, she would bow graciously.

Jo poked her in the back. "Snap out of it—warmups are starting."

Casey shook her head to clear it of her daydream. "I was just thinking abut winning League. I hope we can do it."

"I'm sure we can. First of all, I'm going to win

the individual trophy on bars," Jo said in a determined voice.

Casey laughed. "Move over, Julianne! Here comes Jo!" Julianne McNamara had been Jo's favorite gymnast since she'd won a silver medal in the 1984 Olympics. Julianne's daring and original moves on the uneven bars had inspired Jo for the last five years, in fact.

Joining Monica on the mat, the girls enthusiastically went through their stretching and warmup exercises. When they were divided into groups, Monica was assigned to the balance beam, her least favorite event.

Casey and Jo would start practice at the vault. When it was her turn, Casey ran down the runway and did a Tsukahara, a difficult twisting somersault. She landed well and felt pleased with herself.

From her place in line, Jo gave her friend a thumbs-up sign.

"Stick with compulsories today!" Bear hollered from across the gym, where he was working with the girls on the balance beam. Casey heard one of the other girls snicker, and she wished she could disappear under the bleachers. He could certainly have told her that without yelling! That had never been his style of coaching before.

As she walked back to her place in line, Casey exchanged looks with Jo and shrugged.

"What's with him?" Jo nodded toward Bear.

Casey shrugged. "Who knows?"

"It was pretty low—yelling at you in front of everybody."

"Maybe he's trying to prove I'm no different from any of the others," Casey said, still trying to understand why her dad had jumped on her.

"Try to ignore it." Jo gave her a punch on the arm. "Your turn again."

This time Casey stuck with the compulsory vault, completing it easily with no steps on her landing. The assistant coach working with her group nodded his approval. She stole a glance at her dad, but he only frowned and looked away.

Casey's group moved to the uneven bars and then to floor exercise. When she finished the last of her three tumbling runs with a strong double back aerial somersault, the girls applauded. She saw her dad look over, his mouth pressed together in a firm line, his eyes cold. She sighed. It didn't look like she was going to get any warm fuzzies from him today.

Casey thought about how much fun it had been to have him as her coach when she was little. He had made it so exciting, encouraging her all the way. *I guess that's all in the past,* she thought. Shrugging, she walked slowly over to the balance beam, dreading having to work with her father. She procrastinated taking her turn, dragging Jo to the back of the line. "With my luck, I'll probably fall off the beam," she whispered.

Abruptly, Bear turned around and scowled at Casey. She blushed. He didn't seem to mind when anyone else talked! But she didn't want to risk him singling her out again, so she simply turned to watch the other gymnasts on the beam.

"Atta girl! Next time just spot something when you make that turn," Bear encouraged Ginny as she almost fell off the beam.

Maybe it won't be so bad, Casey thought, *if he coaches me the same as all the others.* She didn't see why it couldn't work out. But deep down inside she had a nagging feeling it wouldn't, not after what had happened so far that day. He had been so mean to her and so nice to everyone else.

Jo finished her routine, and Bear nodded. "Good work, Jo. We need to work on strengthening that aerial, but it's looking good."

Only when she heard her father's voice did Casey realize she hadn't watched Jo. Now it was her turn. She took a deep breath and walked over to the beam. She carefully did the handstand mount onto the narrow piece of wood.

"More height!" Bear commanded.

Tensing up, Casey lost her concentration in the middle of the routine and wobbled in two places. However, she nailed a high dismount, which she thought would make up for the other errors.

Instead, her father frowned at her. "Benson, you need to concentrate harder!" he snapped.

Benson? she thought. *So that's how he wants it. Well, she could play the same game.* "Yes, Coach," she said in her most formal voice.

A few giggles went through the group, but Bear whirled around and squelched them with a fierce look. He stared at Casey a minute and then turned to the next girl. "Let's run through those again."

At the end of practice, Casey was thoroughly discouraged and she went through the series of strength exercises only halfheartedly. After sit-ups, and pull-ups on the bars, Bear assigned twenty-five handstand push-ups. The girls had the choice of doing them against a wall, or having another girl hold their feet. Monica and Jo had teamed up together, so Casey started toward the wall by herself.

"Do you need a partner?" Jill Ramsey asked, coming up behind her.

Casey turned around to find the senior girl smiling at her. After such a tough afternoon, it was nice to see someone friendly. "Sure, why not?" she said.

They found a free spot on the mat. "You go first," Jill instructed Casey.

She caught Casey's ankles as Casey kicked up into a handstand. *Trust Dad to like these,* Casey thought, breathing hard as she lowered herself up and down while Jill counted to twenty-five.

They switched, and Casey steadied Jill while she completed her set of handstand push-ups. When they had finished, Jill said hesitantly, "Casey? You know, the first day of practice is always the worst." She patted her on the back.

It sure is, Casey thought, *especially when you're the coach's daughter.* But she knew Jill had heard the way her father had yelled at her, and that she was only trying to cheer her up. "Thanks. I hope so," she said softly, trying to smile.

Several of the newer girls finished the push-ups and promptly started heading for the locker room. Bear blew his whistle and motioned for them to return. "Sorry, girls. Because other teams practice here, we have to put all the equipment away every night." He laughed. "Guess who gets to do that!" A protest went up from the gymnasts, but Casey noticed the older girls had already started hauling the mats toward the storage area.

Casey and Monica rolled the vault toward the wall while Jo dragged the springboard behind them. Since the three of them worked out at a private club, they were used to such long, hard practices, but some of the other gymnasts looked exhausted.

Monica and Jo were discussing the first workout at length. Casey walked into the locker room ahead of them. At the moment she didn't want to talk to anyone, not even her best friends.

She sighed. As she had predicted, it was not going to be easy working with her dad. He had proved in one practice that she wouldn't get any special favors. She didn't want favors—she just wanted the same fair treatment the others got. But today she had certainly been coached differently from anyone else!

Chapter 6

★ ★ ★ ★ ★ ★ ★ ★ ★ ★

SATURDAY morning Casey slept in until nine o'clock. When Tom's stereo finally woke her, she stretched her arms over her head and enjoyed the luxury of not having to get up. Outside, a maple tree scraped its red and yellow leaves against her window, making a light, rustling noise.

A beautiful sunny day and she had no school or gymnastics. Casey loved Chicago's fall weather. Gone were the hot, muggy days of July and August, and the wind, snow, and ice wouldn't arrive for a few more months.

She looked around the room she'd had since she was a little girl. It had gone through two decorating changes in the last five years, but Casey loved its current look. She'd chosen the rose print fabric herself. From her bed she glanced at the ruffled curtains that framed the large window overlooking the backyard. If she stood on a chair she could see Lake Michigan off in the distance. In grade school she had told her friends that her bedroom had a lake view.

Large posters of Mary Lou Retton and Hope Spivey decorated her closet door. She looked at the girls and wondered if she'd ever be good enough to get a poster made of herself. If she made Elite next spring, she'd be on her way. She closed her eyes and tried to decide what pose she'd choose if it ever happened to her.

Thinking about gymnastics reminded her of the day before. Why had her dad treated her so harshly all week? she wondered. She knew he had to be fair to the others, but this was ridiculous! They'd always gotten along well. Casey smiled. As long as she didn't goof off in gymnastics, they'd gotten along well. But she *had* been working hard. As much as she dreaded it, she would have to ask him about it—without sounding as if she wanted special treatment from him.

She heard the front door close and then the car pull out of the driveway. She knew her mom and dad were leaving for their weekly Saturday morning tennis match. Casey thought about how much her mom loved tennis, and how she had transferred that love for the sport to Casey's older sister. After many years of lessons Barbara had won the number two singles spot on the varsity team.

At ten o'clock Casey finally pulled herself out of bed. She always spent Saturday afternoons with Monica and Jo, and Jo had said she would call about noon. All she had to do first was dust and vacuum, her weekly chores.

"Vacuuming, yuck!" she said aloud to Mary Lou Retton on the wall. "When I have my own house, I'm going to have enough money to hire a maid."

She ambled down to the kitchen to find Tom half buried in the refrigerator. "Anything *good* to eat around here?" he asked as he rummaged through the shelves.

"Probably not," Casey said in what she hoped

was her most indifferent voice. She didn't feel like being nice to Tom after the way he'd acted toward her at school. On two more occasions he'd belted out Tarzan yells while his friends laughed. She'd never forgive him for that.

"Mom and Dad's definition of food is a far cry from the rest of the world's." He stacked milk, juice, and eggs on the counter. "Just once I'd like to open the fridge and have it bulging with junk food." He gave the door a slam and picked up the carton of milk. He drained it in one long gulp. Then he picked up the juice.

"Hey, save some of that for me—*please*," Casey demanded.

Tom lowered the juice jar from his mouth and shoved it across the counter toward her. "What's the matter with you? Wake up on the wrong side of the bed or something?"

Casey grabbed a glass from the cupboard and poured herself some juice. She turned away from her brother. "I don't even want to talk to you," she said.

"What'd I do?"

Casey whirled around. "How can you ask that? After you did all those stupid Tarzan yells in front of the whole school!"

"Aw, come on, Cheetah. It was just in fun."

"It's not fun!" Casey protested. "And don't call me by that name anymore!"

Tom leaned back against the stove and gave her a lazy smile. "Well, well, Little Miss Gymnastics Team! Aren't you high and mighty. I heard you were acting pretty snobby, but this is ridiculous."

"Me! Where'd you hear that? From those dumb senior girls on the team who won't even talk to me?" Casey felt her face turn red. She hated to let him see how mad he could make her.

Tom gave her another smile. "Maybe they think *you're* stuck up."

"Stuck up! You make me so mad! Dad's being a real dork to me in the gym and you're . . . oh, just leave me alone," Casey said as she stormed out of the kitchen.

"What's this about Dad?" Tom called after her. "Tell me!"

Casey ran upstairs to her room, slammed the door, and threw herself on the bed. How could he possibly think all those Tarzan yells were fun. Maybe for him they were.

And stuck up? The girls were saying that because her dad was the coach—because they didn't like her. She put her face in her pillow and let the tears flow. Why couldn't they accept her as just another member of the team?

A half hour later she got up and took her shower, determined not to let Tom ruin her whole Saturday. The hot water pounded away her frustrations, and she was able to think about the afternoon at the Northwestern swimming pool with Monica and Jo. She looked at her pale arms. Too bad they hadn't planned one last time at the beach. Oh, well, October was too late for a tan anyway.

She put on her beige shorts and jungle-print blouse over her swimsuit. Avoiding Tom, she went down to the closet, where her mom kept the cleaning supplies. She decided to dust first. There was always the chance that some major catastrophe would happen and she wouldn't have to vacuum. She giggled. Maybe Chicago would have an earthquake—or a tidal wave.

Running the dustcloth across the tops of the tables, she quickly finished the living room. Before she put the supplies away, she went back and dusted the bottom chair rungs in the dining room. Her mom always checked there to see if she'd done a thorough job.

As she finally hauled the vacuum from the closet, Tom came down the stairs. "What's going on between you and Dad at the gym?" he asked again.

Casey ignored him and flipped the switch on the vacuum. She'd decided never to speak to him again. A minute later she sneaked a look behind her, but he was gone.

When she'd finished her chores, she started hunting for her beach towel so she could pack her bag to take to the pool. She stuffed in her brush and shampoo, and then at the last minute tossed in her Walkman. When Jo phoned, she was ready to leave.

"Hi, Casey. Are you all set?" Jo's excited voice came over the line. "There's a bus at twelve-ten. Can you make it?"

Casey looked at the clock. "Give me five minutes and I'm out of here."

"Meet you at the bus stop," Jo said.

Casey grabbed her bag and took the stairs two at a time. As she hurried out the front door, she almost ran right into her father. "Oops, sorry, Dad."

"Hi, sugar! Your mom just dropped me off. She's going shopping. Where are you off to?" Mr. Benson asked, setting his tennis bag on the hall floor.

Uh-oh, Casey thought. She was in too big a hurry to talk about gymnastics now. "I'm going to the pool with Jo and Monica."

"Time for lunch first?"

"We're going to eat before we go swimming," Casey said as she took a step toward the door. "But don't worry, I won't get a stomach cramp. We'll wait for an hour first."

Mr. Benson headed for the kitchen. "Come in here for a minute. You can tell me about your plans."

Casey took a quick glance at her watch. She could spare about ten minutes and then she'd have to split. Reluctantly, she joined her dad. She didn't understand it. He was acting as if nothing had happened between them.

"How did Monica and Jo like their first week of workouts?" He took a package of hot dogs out of the refrigerator.

"*They* liked it fine." She hesitated. This wasn't the best time, but he was the one who had brought up the subject. "Dad, didn't you kind of ... well ... make it hard on me?" She held her breath, waiting for his answer.

Her father's smile faded. "I wasn't treating you any differently, Casey. But you are going to have to work hard on my team."

Casey shrugged. They obviously hadn't seen practice in the same way. She decided to wait and see how the second week went. "Look, Dad, I have to catch the bus. I'll see you later."

Mr. Benson studied her, then shook his head. "All right, have a good time." Almost as an afterthought, he called after her, "Eat something decent!"

"I'll get a sprouts burger!" she yelled as she dashed out the door and started running for the bus stop.

As she got nearer, she saw Jo and Monica waving frantically at her. "Hurry!" Jo cried.

Casey arrived just as the bus came around the corner and coughed to a halt. "My dad got home just as I was leaving. He wanted to chat," Casey explained. She rolled her eyes.

"We thought you were going to miss the bus," Monica said as they headed to the back, where there was room for them to sit together. Casey sank down on the seat and closed her eyes.

"What's wrong with you?" Jo asked as she dropped into the seat next to Casey.

Casey sighed. "I've had enough family encounters for a month. Good thing Mom was out shopping or we'd probably have gotten into it, too."

"What happened?" Monica passed each of them some red licorice strips. "I know this isn't your dad's idea of a good snack."

Jo took two pieces. "Yeah, but it's Saturday. Let's live a little. Go on, Casey, tell us what happened."

Casey reached for the candy. "I yelled at Tom this morning about those dumb Tarzan yells." She took a deep breath. "He said the other girls think I'm stuck up."

Jo wrinkled her nose. "He's crazy!"

"He's only saying it to make you mad." Monica leaned across Jo and gave Casey another piece of licorice. "Just ignore him and he'll cut it out eventually."

Jo laughed. "But remember, this advice comes to you from someone with absolutely no experience dealing with brothers."

"Well, it's still good advice." Monica gave Jo a dirty look. "I'm sure Tom made it all up anyway."

"I hope so," Casey said, and concentrated on chewing the sticky red licorice. If her teammates thought she was a snob and her coach thought she was lazy, it was going to be a horrible season!

Later that day, after trying to outdo each other on the diving board, the three girls sat on the edge of the pool.

Monica rubbed her stomach. "Ohh, that last one was a real ouch."

Casey laughed, splashing her feet in the water. "At least water is softer than a mat."

"Hey, Casey, did your dad say anything about workout?" Jo asked.

"Yeah, how come he's being so tough on you?" Monica added.

"He doesn't think he was any harder on me than he was on you or anyone else." Casey paused and looked at her friends. "Did he treat us the same? Am I imagining things? Is this idea of mine all up here?" Casey tapped her head.

"No way! Anyone could tell he was down on you," Jo said, rubbing her leg to keep warm.

"He was really nice to me," Monica added.

"Let's not talk about it anymore." Casey jumped into the water. "Come on, I'll race you to the end." Taking off before her friends could react, she started racing down the pool.

Once she made it to the shallow end, Casey flipped over onto her back and pretended she'd been waiting for hours, just floating in the water. "What kept you?" she asked nonchalantly as Monica and Jo swam up beside her.

Monica paused to catch her breath. "Hey, Casey, you haven't told us how you like art class. Have you created any museum pieces yet?" she teased.

Casey smiled, and wondered if she should tell them about Brett. She had had a lot of fun with him in class and hoped they'd get to be better friends, but she didn't want Monica and Jo to laugh at her crush. Usually, she shared everything, but now she wondered if she should.

"You have a funny look on your face," Jo said. "So I know you're not telling us something."

"What is it? Is it a guy?" Monica probed.

"It's nothing! Just my table partner, Brett. He's showing me how to make stuff with clay."

Monica smiled and raised one eyebrow. "So you guys have to work *closely* together, right?"

"Casey!" Jo slapped her on the arm. "Why didn't you say anything? We're your best friends."

"Look, you guys, it's nothing. He's just a guy who sits next to me in class," Casey maintained. "Besides, we've been so busy with gymnastics that it just didn't seem important."

A teasing look came into Monica's eyes. "Well, if *you* don't want him . . ."

"No, he's too short for you, Monica," Casey told her friend, thankful that Brett was only about five foot ten. "You like only those tall basketball players."

Monica splashed Casey. "I was just kidding. I'd never try to take away your guys."

Jo rested her back against the ladder on the side of the pool. "Maybe he has some friends he could introduce us to—cute friends."

"Cut it out, you guys! I don't even know him that well."

"Yeah, but we can tell you'd like to." Monica laughed and started swimming back to the deep end.

"Go for it, Casey," Jo said seriously. "It would be great to have a boyfriend."

Casey sighed. "It would be. But with gymnastics, I probably wouldn't have time."

Jo nodded in agreement. "Well, we can always dream."

Chapter 7

★ ★ ★ ★ ★ ★ ★ ★ ★ ★

STANDING at the corner of the spring floor Monday afternoon, Casey waited for the music to begin. For the last two weeks she had struggled through the gymnastic workouts, trying to perform as well as her father expected her to. But no matter how hard she tried, it never seemed good enough for him.

When the first notes sounded, she started her optional floor exercise by jumping into a dive roll. The first part of her routine went well, but as she got ready for her second tumbling run, she noticed her dad had joined the assistant coach on the sidelines. She felt her body tense. Why did he have to watch her every move? Why couldn't he leave her alone and pretend that she was just another gymnast?

Casey ran diagonally across the floor and finished her tumbling run with a double back aerial somersault. Unfortunately, she had gained too much momentum, and she overrotated. She lost her balance and sat down on the mat. She quickly scrambled up and continued the routine, but each time she passed her dad, she could see how disappointed he was with her.

"A dual meet on Thursday, and she can't even stay on her feet," she heard him mutter as he returned to the beam.

On bars it was even worse. Regardless of how well Casey did, her father found something to dislike, and snapped at her across the room for the little things that he ignored in other gymnasts. Furious, Casey gritted her teeth and continued through the workout. She was determined not to lose her temper in front of the other girls. But what made the whole afternoon even worse were the smiles on the faces of some of the older girls. It was as if they were enjoying Casey's humiliation.

Jo managed to slip over once or twice during practice to give Casey a little hug of support. Even the assistant coach noticed Bear's continuous nagging, and at one point questioned his head coach's comments with a raised eyebrow.

But Coach Benson merely shrugged and went back to the group on the balance beam.

When practice ended, Casey stormed over to the mats for strength exercises. She raced through her sit-ups and then waited for Jill to finish. Since the first workout when Jill had asked to be her partner, they had continued to pair up.

Over at the bars her father was busy supervising Jo and Monica on their pull-ups. When he happened to look at her, Casey turned away.

Jill completed her sit-ups, and they started the push-ups. Casey almost knocked Jill over when she kicked up into a handstand. "I'm sorry," she said, "but he makes me so mad."

"He's not being fair." Jill caught Casey's ankles and steadied her.

Casey didn't answer. She felt like crying, but she wasn't about to let that happen—not in front of the rest of the team.

When they changed positions, Jill squeezed Casey's arm. "I'm sorry," she said. "Maybe it will be better tomorrow."

Casey held Jill's slim ankles and counted out the push-ups. *She's so nice,* Casey thought. *Maybe it's not all because of Tom.*

When Jill finished her handstand push-ups, Casey asked somewhat abruptly, "Are you interested in my brother?" She had to know, one way or the other.

A blush crept up Jill's neck. "I've always thought your brother was nice—and very good-looking." She studied Casey for a minute. "Why? Don't you want me to like him?"

"It's not that. It's just . . . well, a lot of senior girls have been very friendly to me, but all they want to talk about is Tom," Casey explained.

"I see," Jill said. "And you think I'm trying to get to him, too."

"Are you?" Casey asked.

Jill smiled and linked her arm through Casey's. "I can't say I wouldn't love a date with Tom Benson. Anybody would. But I sure don't want to get it through you. I just like being on the team together. You're fun to work with. Okay?"

Casey sighed with relief. She liked Jill—and she believed her, too. Now she could stop worrying about her motives and just accept her friendship. "Yeah, okay." She smiled at Jill. "I'm glad *someone* at workout likes me."

On their way to the locker room they ran into Jo and Monica, who offered their sympathy for the horrible practice session Casey had had. Neither could understand why Casey's dad would be so supportive to them and then yell at Casey. She *was* one of the best. It hadn't taken the three freshmen long to figure out that all those hours of practice with Chip at the Flyaway Gym Club had given them an advantage over their teammates.

"You can sure see how the older girls might resent us," Monica said.

"It's not fun anymore," Casey said, shaking her head. "I never thought gymnastics could be like this . . . with Dad yelling at me and having to worry about the rest of the team liking us."

"At least we have the dual meet this week," Jo said, trying to cheer up Casey. "You'll do great!"

Monica brightened. "That's right! We've got to beat Newman High!"

"They finished really well last year," Jo added. "So we'll have to be tough."

Casey sighed. "I wish we were competing with Chip as our coach."

"Come on, Casey." Jo put an arm around her friend's shoulders. "It can't get any worse. When we beat them on Thursday, maybe he'll lay off."

"I guess you're right," she told them. Casey tried to smile, but inside she had a feeling that even if she won the meet single-handedly, it might not help her relationship with her dad. A perfect ten probably wouldn't be good enough for him!

Thursday afternoon Casey met Monica and Jo in the locker room. For the first time the three freshmen would get to wear their new Fairfield team leotards. Casey looked down at the gold stretchy Lycra fabric of one sleeve that also ran in a diagonal across the front. The other sleeve was royal blue. "I love it!" she cried.

Monica looked at herself in the mirror. "They're terrific!" she agreed.

"They even make me look taller," Jo said, standing on tiptoe.

The three posed together, admiring their reflections. They made quite a trio, Casey thought; she and Jo on either side of the taller Monica. "Let's go!" she said enthusiastically, and they ran out into the gym to join their teammates.

The warmup period allowed each girl to practice her routine on every piece of equipment. The three freshmen stuck together during warmups, encouraging each other as they completed each apparatus; they went through each routine once, and then carefully repeated the harder portions.

A few students straggled in to see the meet, but for the most part it was parents who came to watch. Mr. Benson had tried to build an interest in the team by encouraging other students to support them, but few ever attended the events.

Casey smiled as she saw her mom slip in and sit off to one side. Mom—always there. Not only for Casey, but because she loved all sports.

She turned to find Jill standing behind her. "Do you think we'll beat them?" Casey asked.

"I hope so. But I know from last year that they have one girl who's super on vault—and a couple who are pretty good on bars."

"Jo can handle the bars." Looking at the other girls practicing, Casey didn't think there was anyone who could beat her friend.

When warmups were finished, Bear called his team together to assign their lineups. When he announced Monica would be going last on the floor exercise, Casey nodded her approval. Since the scores tended to build as the competition went along, a coach always put the girl he thought would do best in the final spot.

Casey ended up with third place on both vault and floor exercise, which was fine with her. But then Bear put Jo at number two on the uneven bars. *That was a wrong move*, she thought. The girl who would go last was definitely not as good as Jo. "I don't believe it!" she whispered to her friend.

Disappointment flooded Jo's face, but then she shrugged. "I'll still beat them all," she said confidently.

Casey smiled at her friend. She admired Jo's intense desire to win. She always inspired Casey to try a little harder, to give a routine everything she had.

When Bear read the balance beam order, Casey was surprised—as well as puzzled—when she was named last. Though it was her best event, she had to question his logic. How could he complain about her constantly yet still think she had the best chance of getting the top score on beam?

Casey ended up in a group with Jo to start the meet at the vault. "This is perfect!" Jo whispered. "Vault will give us a chance to shake out the tension."

"Who's tense?" Casey clenched her fists and teeth and rolled her eyes in fake terror.

Jo giggled. "One thing about you, Casey, you always make me laugh." Her smile faded. "And I need that today."

Casey draped her arm over Jo's shoulders. "Relax, it's only a dual meet. It's nothing compared to the Elite Championships."

"I know." Jo nodded and then got up for her turn. "Well, here goes nothing."

Jo completed a good vault and returned for her second try. When she finished, it was obvious by her grin that she was satisfied with her first event.

After putting resin on her gymnastic shoes, Casey stepped up to begin her vault. She raised her arm to salute the judge. Since a gymnast's run determines the rest of the vault, Casey raced down the runway, picking up a lot of speed before she did her hurdle onto the springboard. The feeling of momentarily floating through space thrilled her as she completed the twists in the air. When she came down solidly on the mat behind the vault, she knew it had been a good one. The judges gave her an 8.6.

Casey looked over at her dad, expecting the same thumbs-up sign he'd often given when she was competing as a child. Instead, all she received was a curt nod.

Her second attempt was not quite as good, but she knew they'd take her first score, which was right in there with the best of them. When her group finished, Casey had beaten the top-seeded girl on her own team. Now she'd have to watch the "super star" from Newman.

Jo and Casey moved to the uneven bars with their group, pausing for a second to ask Monica how she had done on beam. "Ohh," Monica moaned, and grimaced. "You know what my beam's like. I got killed."

"Cheer up," Casey said. "You'll wow them on the floor." She and Jo continued over to the uneven parallel bars.

Casey thought the bars were the most exciting event to watch, and Jo proved her right as she released the low bar to reach the high and casted up to a handstand. Moving quickly and smoothly through the routine, Jo showed off her strength and technique beautifully. When she completed her flyaway layout dismount, all the other gymnasts in the group nodded in approval—except Casey, who grinned at her friend. A 9.1 showed the judges' agreement.

"That was fantastic!" Casey said. She pounded Jo on the back in congratulations.

Jo reached for a towel to wipe the sweat off her face. "It felt great!"

When Casey's turn came, she rubbed chalk on her hands and ran through her routine in her mind before she saluted the judge and swung into her routine. She performed well, but her foot missed the bar and threw off her dismount. Struggling to keep control, she cranked her front somersault around and barely landed upright on the mat. Bars were not her best event, but she had enough difficulty in her routine to score a respectable 7.5.

When they moved to the floor event, Casey sat down near the mat. She looked at the hard calluses on her palms that came from working on the bars. *Not exactly the greatest for hand-holding*, she thought. *Not that anyone's asking me to hold his hand!*

The music drew her attention back to Ginny, who had already started her routine. Floor exercise went well for the group, including Casey, but she knew none of them could beat Monica. In fact, after watching the Newman High girls, she decided Monica had first place all sewn up.

The tension grew for Casey as she reached her last event. She saw her dad walk closer to watch. The balance beam was her specialty, and she wanted to show him how much she could help the team.

Casey punched the springboard and sprang onto the beam. She completed a high stag above the narrow piece of wood. She turned and threw herself into a back handspring, landing solidly. Then she did her pirouette turn and set up for her round-off tuck somersault dismount, which would help score extra points for style and flair. The judges gave her a 9.2, and Jo quickly hugged Casey. "You were so *cool* out there!" she whispered to her.

Still hoping for a positive reaction from her father, after she sat back down on the mat Casey looked around for him. But he had already walked away. She didn't even know if he had seen her whole routine—or her excellent score.

Unfortunately, Jo did not start her balance routine half as well. She wobbled after she mounted the beam. Catching herself, she did a high stag leap but fell off on her next move. Casey shook her head. She could see that Jo was angry with herself, and that was bad for a gymnast. Jo needed to shake it off, forget her mistake, and get back on the beam.

But Jo's concentration had disappeared, and she fell off a second time before she finished her routine.

Shoulders slumped, Jo went off to sit by herself as the judges flashed a score of 5.75. Casey decided to just let her go. For Jo, performing poorly in her first high school meet would be devastating. She was so competitive, and Casey knew she'd want to be alone.

Finally, all the scores were tallied and the winners' blocks were pulled to the middle of the mats. As a team, Fairfield High had easily won the meet.

Casey noticed that her dad was finally smiling. At least now that she'd scored so well, maybe he

would get off her back. He had nothing to complain about anymore. Casey grinned as her name
was called as the individual winner on the balance
beam. She climbed on the blocks, satisfied that
she'd deserved the top score on this event. She
waved at her mom, who stood up to take a picture
of her.

Monica finished first in floor exercise, and the
girl from Newman was way out in front on the
vault. Casey came in behind her, a distant second.
Jo finished first on the uneven bars, but she didn't
smile as she stood on the blocks to receive her
ribbon.

After totaling the scores from each event, the
judges then announced the All-Around winners.
Casey applauded when Jill was called for fifth place
and Ginny for sixth. Monica stopped to hug Casey
on her way up to get the fourth-place ribbon.

Casey held her breath as a girl from Newman
was awarded third place. She knew she had to be
in the top five. Finally, the announcer said, "And
our second-place All-Around winner is Casey Benson!"

Smiling, Casey climbed up on the block, hugging
Monica and her other teammates on the way. Winning always made her pulse race and her heart
beat faster. She had done it! It didn't matter that
the super vaulter from Newman had placed first.
She had showed her team—and her dad—that she
could make a very important contribution to their
win.

When Jo heard that the All-Around scores did
not include her, she stormed off without waiting
for Monica or Casey. Jo had never done so poorly
on beam before, Casey thought, and she had
wanted to win their first meet so badly. If Jo was

going to get a scholarship to pay for her college education, she had to be the best. Her family couldn't afford to send her to college, and gymnastics was the one way she could get there.

As Casey entered the locker room, Jo was pulling her jeans on over her leotard, hurrying to dress before any of the others came in to change and discuss the meet. Obviously hearing her excited teammates on their way in from the gym, Jo grabbed her gym bag, snapped her combination lock shut, and fled out the side door.

Casey truly felt sorry for her friend as she watched Jo's hurried departure. She had started out so well that afternoon. Casey sighed. It was always the same. Whenever Jo did poorly she shut the others out. Why, Casey wondered, did Jo let gymnastics get in the way of their friendship?

Casey shook her head and started to change her clothes. For her, the meet had been a big success. Not only had she proved to the seniors that she was good enough to be on the team, she had shown them she could make it on her own, without her dad's help.

Even better, she had helped Fairfield win, and her dad had to be happy about that. Maybe now he would let up on her and they could go through the rest of the season on good terms.

Chapter 8

"MICHELANGELO! It's incredible!" Brett Kelly clutched his blond curly hair, pretending to pull it out. "Uh . . . what is it?"

Casey surveyed the lump of red clay she'd been shoving around her desk for a week. It really didn't look like anything, she decided. She'd started out to make a gymnast doing a backbend, but it had ended up looking like a horseshoe instead. So she had started all over again—with equally disastrous results. "It's a duck," she told Brett.

"A what?" Brett looked at the would-be duck and groaned. "If we don't make this look like something before quarter grades, you'll be a dead duck!"

As horrible as she felt about the mess in front of her, Casey liked the way he said "we." Together they might make something out of it. She glanced at his project.

In front of Brett, his sculpture stood finished. A girl sitting on a rock stared into space with a dreamy look on her face. How could he make it look so real? she wondered, glancing again at her attempt.

Casey shook her head. "I guess I'm just not artistic."

"I'll second that," Brett said.

"What should I do?" she asked.

"I know what you could make." Brett studied her clay with a serious expression, but the corners of his mouth twitched as if he were about to start laughing.

Casey poked at the clay. "Whatever it is, it'll have to be easy."

"Oh, it is," he assured her, a grin spreading across his face. "You can make a football!"

Casey stared at Brett. Was he serious?

When he saw her surprised reaction, Brett started laughing and fell into his chair. "Don't you need a Christmas present for Tom this year?"

There it was—her brother again. Why did everybody have to know Tom? Casey turned away and began pounding the clay back into one big chunk so she could start again.

"Casey," Brett said softly, "you're not mad at me, are you?"

When he gave her his best "sad puppy" look, she knew she couldn't stay angry at him. "No, I'm not."

"Good! Then how about going to the Halloween dance with me?"

Brett had actually asked her to a dance! She did a quick mental check to see if there was any reason she couldn't go. When she was working out with Chip, she had always had to stay too late— but the high school program finished at seven-thirty. And there wasn't a meet that day, either. She could go!

"Well," Brett asked, "did you get Super Glue in your mouth or something?"

Casey started laughing, realizing she hadn't given him an answer yet. Brett was the funniest boy she had ever met, and he wanted her to go to the dance with him. Fairfield High wasn't so bad after all. "I'd like to," she said, and suddenly felt embarrassed, standing there looking at him. "Just give me some help with this mess."

Brett grinned. "Okay. How about a dolphin? I did that for my very first project."

Casey nodded and Brett showed her how to form a base that resembled waves in motion. She worked diligently for the rest of the period. When it was time to clean up, Casey was elated. Not only had Brett asked her to the Halloween dance, but she felt better about her project than she had all week. Maybe she'd have something to turn in after all.

Casey could hardly wait for the morning to end. Both Jo and Monica had classes in the other wing, so she'd had to wait until lunchtime to share her good news. Fidgeting through algebra, she found it hard to concentrate, and in English she spent the hour gazing out the window, dreaming about the dance. Her braces would even be off by then.

When the bell rang, she snapped back to reality and quickly copied down the homework assignment. She made it to her locker before Monica and Jo, and she threw her books inside, trying to act cool—as if nothing special had happened. What she really wanted to do was jump up and down and tell everyone. She could hardly stand it! She was going to burst!

A few minutes later Jo and Monica walked down the hall toward her, deep in conversation. Tossing "coolness" aside, Casey slammed her locker shut and ran up to meet them. Grabbing them both in a bear hug, she started giggling.

"What's wrong with you?" Monica asked. She stepped back from Casey.

"You guys!" Casey squealed. "It's happened! Brett asked me to the Halloween dance!"

Soon the three were hugging again, oblivious to everyone passing by in the hallway.

Monica finally untangled herself from their embrace. "So much for freshman sophistication."

"Let's get out of here." Jo gently pushed Casey back toward her locker, out of the path of other students.

"Ohh, I'm so excited. I didn't think he'd really ask me," Casey said.

"That's great," Monica agreed, but she sounded less than happy about it.

Casey was confused. "Monica, what's wrong?" she asked.

"I guess I'm just disappointed. Now we won't be going together, after we'd planned the costumes and everything."

"Oh, that's right!" Jo said, and her smile disappeared, too.

Casey thought of the three Smurf costumes they had assembled, and how they'd planned on going to the dance together. "Maybe someone will ask you, too." Casey hesitated. "I could see if Brett has two friends."

"No, don't worry about it. We'll see you at the dance anyway," Monica assured Casey. "It's okay!"

Jo brightened. "We can still be Smurfs together at school. I heard almost everyone wears costumes here on Halloween."

As the three girls walked to the cafeteria, Casey continued to think about the dance. Even the most exciting moments, it seemed, had some sadness in them. She'd been so thrilled about Brett that she had forgotten her friends and the plans they had made together. Dating would make a big difference in their lives—but a good one. She smiled. It was bound to happen to all of them, but being the first one asked out ... well, breaking up the trio was hard.

She shook her uncertainty away by thinking about Brett and how much fun he would be on a date. *The Halloween dance is going to be the best evening of my life,* Casey told herself. *And nothing is going to spoil it.*

That afternoon Casey went into the locker room hopeful that the tension between her and her dad would ease up soon. Lately, things seemed to be snowballing. Instead of improving with all the hours of practice, Casey felt as if she were getting worse. She couldn't concentrate because she was too busy worrying about what her father would think of her performance. Especially after last night!

She thought about the stormy scene they'd had at home after the meet. Sure that he'd be happy about the win—and her first place on the balance beam—Casey had practically floated into the kitchen for dinner. Her mom and dad were already at the table, but Tom's place was empty. Because he had football practice, he usually ate later in the evening. Casey wished he were there to hear about how well she'd done at the meet—then maybe he'd stop treating her like a little kid.

"Great meet, Dad!" Casey said cheerfully as she helped herself to a serving of the huge green salad. When he didn't answer, she looked up, sur-

prised. Mr. Benson's face did not look like that of
a winning coach's. "Yes, but this was an easy meet.
Besides, this one really doesn't count. Newman isn't
even in our league. The next ones will be tougher,"
he said.

"We'll beat everyone!" Casey told him confidently.

"Don't be so cocky," Bear admonished her.
"We're not guaranteed to win anything, considering the way you performed today."

"What?" Casey dropped her fork. "But I won the
beam and finished second All-Around."

"Maybe so, but you're still not working up to
your ability. You'd think after all these years, you'd
be able to concentrate," he commented.

"Now, Bear, don't be so critical," Mrs. Benson
warned her husband, obviously trying to smooth
things over. She started passing the serving dishes
around for second helpings.

"Concentrate!" Casey jumped to her feet. "How
can I concentrate when you're always picking on
me? Why don't you just leave me alone!"

As she ran out of the kitchen, Casey heard her
mother say, "Don't you think you were a little hard
on her?"

Now, back at school, she still shuddered when
she thought about the way her father had told her
she wasn't working up to her ability. She was trying as hard as she could, and his attitude wasn't
helping. Didn't he know he was making her life
miserable? Fortunately, when Casey went into the
gym, she found that the assistant coach would be
in charge of workout that afternoon. Her dad had
gone to a district coaches meeting.

Relieved, Casey enjoyed practice for the first
time since she had made the team.

* * *

Saturday morning Casey hopped out of bed excited that she and Jo were going to spend the day at the beach. It would be the last time this year. The weather was starting to get cold, and it was already too late to swim in Lake Michigan.

Casey showered and went downstairs for breakfast. She poured herself a bowl of bran cereal and sighed. Her mom was so health conscious. Even as a child Casey hadn't been allowed to have sugar-coated cereal. *Just once,* she thought, *I'd like to find a box of Cap'n Crunch in the cupboard.*

The phone rang and Tom grabbed it upstairs before it could ring twice. *Probably another girl calling to tell him how well he played last night,* she thought as she took a bite of the soggy flakes. She wondered if it was one of the girls who had invited her to eat at her table in the cafeteria.

"Hey, Cheetah! It's for you!" Tom hollered. "Let me know when you're off. I'm expecting another call."

Casey grimaced at the pet nickname. At sixty he would probably still call her that. She ran up to her room and grabbed the phone. "Hello?"

"I can't go!" Jo wailed. "I'm chained to my bedroom. Mom says I have to get this place dug out today."

"But we'd planned this all week," Casey protested. "Can't you convince her to wait until tomorrow?"

"I tried, but she's wearing her do-it-or-else look."

"How long will it take? Can't you just shove a lot of it under your bed?" Casey asked.

Jo giggled. "Mom's one step ahead of me. She caught me doing that last time, so I really have to clean it today." She sighed. "It's going to take me all day."

"I didn't think it looked *that* bad," Casey said.

"It doesn't—not to me. But Mom's in one of her Mrs. Clean moods," Jo grumbled. "And Dad threatened to hire a bulldozer to deal with the mess."

Casey laughed in spite of herself. "Okay, but you're *sure* there's no way?"

"I'm sorry, Casey. I'll call you when I pass the white-glove test."

After hanging up the phone, Casey wandered around downstairs, dusting the furniture. Monica was at her grandmother's house for the weekend. She didn't want to go to the beach by herself.

Passing the hall mirror, Casey caught a look at her sad, gloomy reflection and laughed. *Is that really me? What a sad-looking character!* And she did have something exciting to look forward to, she thought as she grinned in the mirror. She was getting her braces off late that afternoon! No more metal-mouth!

Casey decided to kill time by working on her English report. Even homework would be better than sitting around feeling sorry for herself.

As she headed upstairs, the phone rang again. She didn't bother to answer it, since it was always for Tom.

"Chee—hey, Casey! It's for you!" he yelled.

Casey noticed with satisfaction that Tom hadn't called her that awful name for once. Maybe she was finally getting through to him. In her room she picked up the phone, expecting to find Jo on the other end.

"Hi, Casey. This is Jill Ramsey. You know, from the team?"

Casey caught her breath. Jill? Calling her? The

senior girl had been so friendly at school, and they'd continued to pair up for strength exercises, but to hear her on the phone was a surprise. "Jill? Hi!"

"I was on my way to the mall, and decided I didn't want to go alone. You interested?"

"The mall? Sure, I'd like that."

"How soon can you leave?" Jill asked.

Casey looked down at her cutoff jeans and bare feet. "Give me a few minutes to change. Oh, one other thing—I have to be back by four-thirty. I'm getting my braces off."

"That's great! All right, I'll pick you up in half an hour."

Casey quickly grabbed a beige denim miniskirt and a matching blouse with a teddy bear print on it. She slipped on her favorite sandals. She looked at her outfit in the mirror. Seniors probably didn't wear teddy bears. She took off the blouse and put on an oversize green T-shirt.

On her way downstairs she poked her head in Tom's room. He was sprawled on top of his bed, listening to his stereo. "Tom!" she yelled over the music.

He turned down the volume. "Yeah, what's up?"

Casey looked around at the shelves lined with trophies. Tom had done well in every sport he'd ever played, and his room showed off his success. "Do you know a girl named Jill Ramsey?"

"Blond? Senior? On the gymnastics team?" When Casey nodded, he raised an eyebrow. "I know who she is. She's in a couple of my classes. Why do you want to know?"

She hesitated. "Just wondered if you were interested in her."

"I don't know her *that* well. Why?"

Casey smiled. "I'm going to the mall with her. I just wanted to make sure you weren't dating her." Casey turned to leave.

"Hey, Cheetah! I mean Casey!" he corrected himself. "Come back here." He rolled to a sitting position. "Why are you hanging around with Jill? What happened to Monica and Jo and the terrible trio?"

"They're busy. And I'm going because she asked me," she said over her shoulder as she left the room. "Please tell Mom where I am and tell her I'll be back to go to the orthodontist at four-thirty."

"Yes, ma'am!" Tom saluted her and lay back down on his bed.

Fifteen minutes later a car horn honked. Casey ran outside and started laughing. Jill had pulled up in front in an open jeep.

"Don't tease me," Jill said. "It's my brother-in-law's. My sister lent it to me for the day because—well, it's a long story. Get in."

Both girls started giggling when Jill tried three times to get the jeep into first gear. "At least you have wheels," Casey said once they were out on the street. None of her other friends were old enough to even have a driver's license. Jeep or not, it was better than taking the bus.

They parked a long way out in the mall lot so that Jill wouldn't have to find reverse gear, and then they headed into the mall.

"This is fun!" Casey said as they headed for the dance wear shop. "I'm glad you called. I was beginning to feel sorry for myself. Jo's mother axed our plans to go to the beach—"

"I *love* Lake Michigan," Jill interrupted. "My uncle has a house near the beach. When I go there, he lets me use his Hobie Cat. Have you ever been sailing?"

"No, I never knew anyone who had a boat. Besides, I've always been too busy with gymnastics," Casey explained.

"You go to Flyaway, don't you? What's that like?" Jill asked.

"Oh, you'd love it! Chip is a great coach!" Casey's voice rose with enthusiasm. Then she realized what she had just said. "I mean, Dad's a good coach, too."

Jill smiled. "He's great as far as I'm concerned. But I can understand how you might feel about him. I still think things will cool down between you, though. Hang in there," she advised. "My first year wasn't exactly fun either!"

The talked about the other team members' strengths as they wandered toward the dance shop, stopping to look in all the store windows. A display of G.I. Joe dolls in a jeep sent them into another laughing attack.

At the dancewear store Jill found the new red leotard she wanted, with Hawaiian print insets. "Isn't this the wildest?" she asked as she modeled it for Casey.

Casey nodded. "It goes great with your blond hair." She tried on several leotards, too, but decided she had more than enough at home—at least for now.

After Jill paid for her leotard, they headed for the frozen-yogurt shop. "No trip to the mall ever seems right without this," Casey said as she plunged her spoon into a double dish of chocolate mixed with peanut butter candies.

The afternoon went by quickly, and when Jill dropped Casey off, both agreed that they'd have to do something together again soon. For Casey it felt weird to be spending time with someone other than Monica and Jo, but she was glad she had done it. More than that, she was happy that Jill was her friend. Not *every* senior on the team resented her, at least.

Chapter 9

✦ ✦ ✦ ✦ ✦ ✦ ✦ ✦ ✦

CASEY sat cross-legged on her bed, staring out the window at the gray sky. She propped her chin in her hands and pressed her nose against the cool glass. A few leaves still clung to the maple tree outside, but their colors had faded like an old corsage.

Casey sighed. On her lap an English book lay open and neglected. Sunday afternoons were too nice to spend on reports. She hated to see October slip by, except that every day brought the Halloween dance closer. Casey smiled at her reflection in the window. She wondered if Brett would notice that she'd gotten her braces off over the weekend.

Casey decided to forget English and go down to the kitchen for an apple. As she reached the top of the stairs, Tom came out from his bedroom. "Wait a minute, Casey! I want to talk to you."

"What do you want to talk about? I don't have anything to say to you," she said bluntly.

Tom rolled his eyes. "Come on, let's call a truce."

Reluctantly, Casey stopped and leaned against the banister. At least he hadn't called her Cheetah. "Okay, I'm listening."

"What's going on between you and Dad?" Tom wanted to know.

"Nothing . . . really. Why?"

"Well, a couple of girls on the team told me you two still had some kind of war going on," he answered.

"What do they do, give you a daily report?" Casey snapped. "Anyway, I thought they'd labeled me a snob. So why should they care?"

Tom laughed. "They did think you were stuck up at first—then they decided they wouldn't want to be in your shoes." Tom sat down on the top step. "Is Dad hard on you?"

"Hard!" Casey studied her brother. Why was he so interested? It had been a long time since they'd talked like friends. She slumped into a bean bag chair, recently ejected from Tom's room into the hallway. "No, he's just ruining gymnastics for me," she said quietly.

Tom paused for a minute. "Maybe you should talk to him about it," he suggested.

Casey frowned. "I should have known you wouldn't understand. *You're* the star! The football hero! And Dad likes his kids to be the best."

"That bad, huh?"

Surprised when Tom didn't answer her outburst with a smart remark, she let out a long sigh. Was he just acting friendly so he could get her to talk— so he could report back to his girlfriends on the team? Or did he really care?

"Why don't you ever come to one of my games?" he suddenly asked.

"How can I?" Casey grumbled. "We don't get out from gymnastics until seven-thirty."

He nodded. "That's right. I forgot. What's the story with Jill Ramsey? You two seem to be good friends."

"Why do you want to know about her?" Casey's eyes narrowed. Did all this brotherly friendliness have anything to do with Jill?

"I saw her when she picked you up yesterday." Tom smiled. "She's real cute."

Casey stood up and stared down at Tom. She didn't want him starting to like Jill. "Just stay away from her," Casey ordered as she started downstairs. "She's *my* friend!"

When she reached the kitchen, she felt guilty. Jill *had* said she'd like a date with Tom, and she knew she could probably get her brother to ask Jill out.

But Casey didn't want that to happen. It would just spoil everything.

On Monday Casey made it to art class early. She had been looking forward all weekend to seeing Brett.

He was already at their table, sitting with his chair tipped back and his feet up. In front of him lay a Snickers wrapper, and he was busy opening a second chocolate bar. "Hi, Michelangelo. What brings you here so early?" He smiled at Casey.

"If you're going to make me into an artist by quarter grades, I thought I'd better hurry up and get started." She motioned to the candy wrappers. "Breakfast?"

Brett grinned. "Want some? It's good for you. Nuts and caramel build strong bones. Energy, too."

"No, thank you." Casey burst out laughing. She couldn't help thinking about what her parents' reaction would be to a chocolate breakfast.

"Hey, you got your braces off!" Brett announced.

"Yeah, on Saturday." Casey beamed, pleased that he had noticed. "How was your weekend?" She hoped it hadn't included any girls.

"Nothing exciting. I just slaved away as usual." Brett reached into a bag at his feet. "I silk-screened a batch of shirts for the French Club." He handed her a turquoise shirt that had been printed with a multicolor logo.

"These are great!" Casey held the shirt up and looked at it more closely. "You did these yourself?"

He reached out to touch the design. "Not bad, huh?"

"You did a terrific job! Do you do this a lot?"

"Whenever." He shrugged, but Casey could see he was pleased by her compliments.

Casey handed him back the shirt. "I'm looking forward to the dance," she said as casually as she could.

"So am I." He smiled sheepishly. "Do you have a costume for it?"

"Not yet," she told him.

Suddenly Brett's face lit up. "Maybe I could make up some shirts."

"Good idea! That way we'll be different from everybody else."

Brett picked up a pad and started sketching. "Just give me a day and I'll show you the design."

Casey pictured how cool they would look in matching shirts. Everyone at the dance would know they had come together. She liked that idea.

"Excuse me, Michelangelo," Brett said, interrupting her daydream, "but if you want to be an artist, you're going to have to actually *work* with that lump of clay in front of you. It's not going to make itself into a dolphin."

Casey giggled. "No, but if it did, it would probably be better than mine!"

* * *

When Casey arrived at the girls' locker room a little later than usual that afternoon, only Jill's friend Ginny was still getting dressed for practice.

In her hurry Casey accidentally knocked Ginny's gym bag off the bench onto the floor. "Sorry, Ginny. I didn't see your bag there," she apologized.

"Oh, it's *you*!" Ginny turned away quickly and kept digging through her locker.

Casey didn't quite understand why she was getting the cold shoulder, but she put the gym bag back on the bench and stuffed a leotard back inside.

"Just leave it alone!" the petite gymnast snapped. She didn't look up from her locker.

"Is something wrong, Ginny?" Casey asked.

"Nothing's wrong with *me*!" Ginny whirled around and stared at Casey a minute. "I just feel sorry for you."

"Me?" Casey smiled. It was nice to know that the other girls were supportive of her when her dad was being so impossible. "Thanks, I really appreciate it, but—"

"Jill is using you so badly," Ginny went on.

Confused, Casey frowned. What did Jill have to do with her father?

"She only wants to get a date with Tom," Ginny said. She pulled her leotard up onto her shoulders and fastened an elastic belt around her waist.

So it was Tom again, Casey thought. "She told me she liked him. But so what? We're friends for other reasons."

"Ha! She's crazy over him! She'd do anything to get him to ask her out—including this phony friendship with you."

Casey felt as if she'd been punched in the stomach. Would Jill really do this to her? All along she'd admitted she liked Tom, but she'd also said she wanted to be Casey's friend first. "She said she wanted to get him by herself," Casey argued, "not through me."

"Sure, sure. And if you believe that . . ." Ginny turned away and stuffed her gym bag inside her locker. Slamming her lock shut, she started to leave. At the gym door she turned around. "She's a senior. There's no way she'd want to be friends with a *freshman* if there wasn't some sort of, shall we say, fringe benefit."

Casey's stomach was churning with anger and hurt, but she forced herself not to show it. She felt tears in her eyes, ready to trickle down her cheeks, but she couldn't show Ginny how much her words had hurt. "I don't believe you," she said softly.

"Fine. But it's the truth. Just think about it," Ginny said as she walked into the gym.

Casey stared at the closed door, feeling very alone. After Ginny's footsteps faded, she crumpled onto the bench. Could it really be true? Were all the friendly overtures from Jill just an act? Was Jill just like all the other senior girls who were nice to her because she was Tom's sister?

Determined not to let the tears come, she finished dressing and then splashed cold water on her face. This was going to be some afternoon. Not only would she have Dad on her back, but now she had Jill to worry about, too.

She went into the gym and walked over to where Monica was stretching on the mat.

"Something's up!" Monica whispered, leaning closer to Casey. "I heard someone in the locker room say something about an extra practice."

Casey began her series of exercises. "Extra? Like on the weekends?"

"I don't know—I sure hope not."

Bear Benson walked into the gym, yelling as he walked. "Girls! Over on the mat!"

"He's smiling," Monica observed.

"Usually that means good news." Casey looked at her dad's face. He wore a big grin, and he was waving a piece of paper in the air.

"Hurry up, everybody, over here!" Bear motioned the girls to the far mat.

Jo dropped down beside Casey. "I got out of class late. What's going on?"

Casey shrugged.

Bear held the paper in front of them. "I've just been informed that we're definitely getting the Olympic tapes I told you about. This is a wonderful opportunity for all of us to learn from the best."

"Will we see them during practice?" Jill asked.

Mr. Benson shook his head. "This weekend we have to share them with Arnold High School. A representative from the distribution company will bring them over after Arnold has finished. So we'll all meet back here Friday night."

"Friday night!" A moan went up throughout the room.

Numbness crept over Casey. "Friday night," she whispered to Jo. "The Halloween dance."

Stunned, the gymnasts looked from one to another. With the gym being used for the dance that night, their practice after school had been shortened for the day. Almost all of them had planned on attending the dance.

Jill was the first to speak. "That's the Halloween dance," she said softly.

Bear looked at his team, who eagerly waited for his reply. He sighed. "We have no choice. The tapes have to go back that night. I'll let you know where and what time we'll meet as soon as I figure that out."

Casey closed her eyes. What else could go wrong? How would she ever tell Brett that she couldn't go to the dance?

How could her dad have done this? Any other time, they'd all have been psyched to see the videos. But now—he'd ruined the evening *and* the tapes.

Bear frowned at his disgruntled team. "Remember, only with true dedication can you reach your goals as gymnasts. This is important—an opportunity to study all the Olympic routines." He looked at the quiet girls. "Now let's get this workout started."

"We don't need a stupid pep talk," Casey muttered under her breath.

Monica gave Casey a look of sympathy, and Jo reached over to squeeze her hand. "Sorry," she whispered.

Casey went through practice halfheartedly. Twice her dad yelled at her to concentrate, but today she knew she was only going through the motions. She just didn't care.

She had looked forward to the dance for days! All her hopes for her and Brett zeroed in on Friday night. And now he was designing their own special costume. If she didn't go with him, who would get to wear her shirt?

Angry at Jill, and depressed about the Halloween dance, Casey did her strength exercises alone against the wall. *This is the worst day of my life,* she thought as she pumped her arms up and down in a handstand push-up. *And it all revolves around this stupid team!*

Chapter 10

★ ★ ★ ★ ★ ★ ★ ★ ★ ★

CASEY lay on her bed and stared at the ceiling. What was she going to do? She still couldn't believe that her dad would really make the team miss the Halloween dance. After all her plans for that night! There had to be some solution.

During dinner Bear tried to start several conversations, but Casey didn't respond. She shoved her food around her plate, but she just wasn't hungry. Finally, after the silence became too much, she excused herself on the pretense of having to study.

Sitting up, she leaned back against the wall as she tried to think of some way to work out the conflict so she could still go to the dance. But no matter how hard she tried, she couldn't come up with any good ideas. She'd just have to go talk to her dad. Maybe she could convince him to find another time. She really wanted to watch the tapes—just not on Friday night.

Finally, Casey worked up the nerve, and she went downstairs to find her father. Outside the door to his study, she felt her courage ebb away. She doubted he'd listen to her argument. Still, she

had to try—for herself as well as for her teammates.

Taking a deep breath, she pushed open the door.
"Dad?" her voice croaked, but she went on. "Can
I talk to you?"

He put down the *International Gymnast* maga-
zine he was reading and smiled. "Okay, sugar. Are
you making progress on your algebra?"

"It's coming along." Casey studied her dad for a
moment, wondering how he could be so pleasant
here at home yet at the gym act like a completely
different person . . . and not a very nice one.

She took another deep breath and crossed her
fingers behind her back. "Dad, I need to talk to
you about the Olympic tapes."

Instantly, his smile disappeared. "Are you going
to try to talk me out of showing them, too?"

"Well, I *was* going to the Halloween dance," she
calmly informed him.

Bear stared at his daughter. He looked horrified.
"Since when is one dance more important than
your gymnastics career? Mary Lou Retton didn't
spend any time going to dances," he reminded her.

Casey looked down at the floor. "Dad, it's the
first time anyone has asked me out! I've always
been too busy with gymnastics to go on dates. I
thought this was the one time I'd—"

Bear held up a hand to silence her. "Casey, you
know what it takes to reach your goal. Gymnastics
is one of the most grueling of sports. It's ded—"

"Forget dedication for once, Dad," Casey coun-
tered. "Try to think about how *we* feel."

Bear jumped to his feet and began to pace across
the study. "I get an unbelievable chance to see
these rare tapes—and no one wants to watch them

with me! What kind of team do I have when even my own daughter would rather go to a party?"

Casey felt like running out of the room, but she forced herself to continue. "Dad, why couldn't we see them Saturday morning?" she reasoned.

Bear stopped pacing and sighed. "The film rep has to pick them up from me first thing Saturday morning, at eight o'clock. They're on a tight schedule. And we're not allowed to copy them, either." Bear paused and took a breath. "There really is no other time."

"But, Dad," Casey argued, "can't we see the tapes two weeks from now? I mean, what difference does it make?"

He stared at her. "What *difference*? Casey, the season will be halfway over by then! And we certainly won't win League with your attitude!" Then abruptly he strode out of the room.

Casey exhaled and flopped into a chair. It was no use. Whatever hope she'd had of changing his mind was gone, along with her chance of going to the dance with Brett. It just wasn't fair.

The next morning Casey peeked into the art room to see if Brett was there. She hated having to face him.

Brett was at their table, but his head was down on his folded arms and he looked as if he were asleep. Casey went in and quietly set her books down. He looked up and yawned. "Hello there. What's the matter? You look like you just read the reviews on your sculpture."

His teasing grin made Casey feel even worse. She couldn't tell him now—maybe after class would be a better time. "Didn't you sleep last night?" she asked as he yawned again.

"I was busy." He went to the cupboard and returned with a new chunk of clay, this time a
creamy white. "Actually, I was working on our
shirts for Friday night."

Oh, no, she thought. *He's going to hate me when
I tell him I can't go.* Casey stood, watching him,
trying to decide what to say first.

Brett looked at her questioningly. "Is the great
Michelangelo taking the day off?" When she didn't
respond, his smile faded. "Hey, something *is*
wrong!"

"Brett," Casey began slowly, her stomach tight-
ening into a knot. "I have some bad news."

He stopped kneading his clay and waited for her
to go on. "Okay, shoot."

"I can't go to the dance with you Friday. I mean,
I can't go at all," she blurted out. Then, relieved
that she had gotten the words out, she sank into
her chair.

Brett stared at her a minute. She could see the
hurt in his eyes, but he quickly turned away. "So
. . . what's the big deal?" he asked, pounding the
clay on the table.

Big deal? she thought. Well, it was a big deal to
her. She tried to tell herself that Brett hadn't meant
that it didn't matter to him. "My dad's making the
whole gymnastics team watch videos of the eighty-
eight Olympics. We're all upset because it's the
night of the dance and I tried to talk him out of it
but he said that—" She stopped, realizing that she
was babbling. "I really wanted to go. I'm sorry,"
she said.

"Yeah. I'm sorry, too," Brett said.

When he returned to his project without saying
anything else, Casey went to get her supplies. She
wished she knew what he was thinking, but it

looked as if Brett was going to keep his opinion to himself.

Throughout class Brett was quiet and Casey didn't ask for any help. She was sure he didn't want anything to do with her. She looked around the room. At least there weren't any open tables, so he wouldn't be able to move. But Casey felt as though Brett had already moved away from her.

The hour ticked past slowly, and Casey felt like smashing her stupid dolphin, but she didn't want to ruin what they had accomplished together. To her surprise, when it was time to clean up, Brett stood back and looked at her emerging sculpture. "How'd you do on your own today?" he asked. Casey remained silent as he surveyed her dolphin with exaggerated seriousness, checking it from all angles. "It's coming . . ." He looked at her and raised an eyebrow. "Whatever you do, don't give up gymnastics."

Casey couldn't help laughing. Brett was so good at breaking the tension. She was so happy that they were laughing together again!

When the bell rang, he reached under his table and pulled out a plastic bag. "You might as well take this with you," he said, handing it to her.

Casey caught her breath as she took the bag. Inside, she could see a bright yellow shirt and part of a wild design. She clutched the bag to her chest. "You finished them. Brett, I really am sorry."

"So am I, Casey." He picked up his books and left the art room.

Casey stared after him. He was so tired because he had stayed up half the night to get their shirts done. The sweetest, funniest, and cutest guy she had ever met—and she had broken her date with him.

Casey wondered if she was truly dedicated to gymnastics, or just crazy.

Friday night the gymnasts arrived at Casey's house to see the videos. Bear had decided to have them at his house because the whole school would be noisy due to the dance. After a few grumbling remarks about the dance, most of the kids seemed to relax and began to laugh and talk. Why couldn't she do that? Casey wondered. Maybe the dance hadn't meant as much to the others. Maybe it wasn't the first time they'd been asked by someone special.

Her father had invited the boys' gymnastics team to join them. They weren't required to come, but a few of them had chosen the tapes over the dance, and their presence made the evening more social.

When Jill arrived, she looked around, and her gaze kept drifting to the stairway, as if she were expecting someone to come down. Although Jill didn't say anything, Casey knew she was hoping Tom would be around. But he was at the dance with the rest of Fairfield High.

Casey had successfully ignored Jill for the past few days, and she didn't want to talk to her tonight, either. Ginny's words kept replaying in her mind. Jill was just using her to get to Tom.

After giving everyone a chance to socialize, Bear called them all into the living room. Casey and Jo found a seat together on the small sofa. "These better be good," Jo muttered.

As they looked at the Olympic performances, Casey could understand why her dad had been so eager to see them. Close-up shots of each gymnast made Casey feel she was there right beside them. It gave her a chance to study the original moves and new variations in the optional routines, and when her dad ran them in slow motion, she could actually figure out how certain moves were done.

When it was over, Casey hated to admit it, but she had been fascinated with the tapes and she was full of new ideas for her own routines. By the excited murmurs in the room, Casey could tell that everybody else had enjoyed them, too.

Jo sighed. "Do you think we'll ever be that good?"

"I saw a couple things I'm going to try," Casey said, wishing she didn't have to wait until Monday to work on the equipment.

"That Russian girl's bar routine was awesome. No wonder she won the gold metal." Jo's eyes sparkled. "Can't you see us on the next Olympic team?"

"We've got three years." Casey wanted to be as optimistic as Jo, but since she had started working with her dad, her Olympic dream had gotten a little clouded. She shook her head. She needed to get back to Chip and start preparing for the Elite Championships.

"Casey! Can you help?"

Casey looked up and saw her mom standing in the kitchen doorway with a tray of apple juice. Casey went to get two large bowls of popcorn and granola.

How embarrassing, she thought. *Would any other high school parties have juice and granola for refreshments? Only if you lived with a nutrition nut!* She wrinkled her nose. Just once she'd like to serve pizza and soft drinks to her friends.

Everyone helped themselves to the food without comment. *I wonder what Brett would think of this snack,* Casey mused. She smiled as she remembered what he'd chosen for his "breakfast of champions."

Thinking of Brett made Casey remember the dance. She curled up on the end of the couch and watched the others. They all seemed to be having a good time, making the best of the evening. Why couldn't she do that? Maybe if it had been just a coach and not her *dad* that had scheduled this video showing and ruined her first date, she could have accepted it.

When the last guests had gone, Casey helped her mother carry the dishes into the kitchen. Mrs. Benson opened the dishwasher and started loading the glasses. "I'm sorry about your dance plans being spoiled," she said.

"Mom, why did this have to happen?" Frustrated, Casey turned away and busied herself putting the leftover granola back into the box. "I wanted to go so much."

Mrs. Benson sighed. "He probably won't say anything to you, but Dad's sorry, too."

"I don't think so, Mom. He doesn't even care!"

Mrs. Benson closed the dishwasher and sat down at the kitchen table. "Don't be too hard on him, Casey. He felt bad for all of you. But it *was* the only time he could get the videos."

"I know, but how would you have felt, Mom?" Casey asked.

Mrs. Benson waited a minute before answering. "I would have died," she admitted.

Casey gave her mom a hug. "Thanks, Mom. I'm going to bed now."

Casey went upstairs and sat down on her bed. She looked out the window at a thin slice of moon that hung over the maple tree. She glanced at her watch. The dance should be ending about now, she thought. She wondered if Brett was with another girl. Had he whipped up another shirt to match his? Oh, why did everything have to turn out like this? If it weren't for the tapes, right now she could have been with him, walking home under that sliver of moonlight. . . .

She rolled off the bed and went to her dresser. Pulling out the knee-length shirt Brett had made for her, she traced her finger over the design and smiled at the loose-jointed skeleton in psychedelic colors. The head of the skeleton was missing from the shirt. She grinned. Knowing Brett, he had probably intended to paint their faces to match.

She undressed quickly, then pulled the shirt over her head and looked at herself in the mirror. In those costumes they certainly would have been different from anyone else. Brett was different from any other boy, too. And he'd chosen to ask *her* to the dance.

Casey felt her eyes start to sting. She closed the blinds so that she wouldn't see the moon, and climbed into bed. With her sleeve she wiped away a stray tear that had trickled down her cheek.

Chapter 11

* * * * * * * * * *

As Casey slipped out the door the next morning, she felt as if she had just won the world championship for speed vacuuming. Quickly she stretched out her muscles, then ran the mile to the Flyaway Gym Club. Chip started classes early, and she was dying to try some of the new things she had seen the night before. But most of all she wanted to talk to Chip about her father.

Once inside the gym, Casey stopped to catch her breath. Chip was spotting a group of nine- and ten-year-old girls on the Class III team, which was one of the first levels of competition. The girls were whispering to one another as they waited in line at the uneven bars. When Chip turned his back, Casey slipped in front of the line.

"Shh!" She signaled to the girls to be quiet, and winked.

"Girls! Quiet down and watch!" Chip called as he helped one of their teammates with her dismount. When he looked up, he grinned and pushed back his Cubs baseball cap. "Well, what have we here? You know, sometimes you do act like a ten-year-old."

Casey growled and charged at him, grabbing him around the waist. He tried to shake her off, but she hung on while the younger gymnasts squealed and cheered.

"Truce! Truce!" Chip yelled, and held up his hands to surrender.

Laughing, Casey let go of Chip and sat down on the mat.

One little girl clapped her hands and chanted, "Casey won! Casey won!"

"Okay," Chip said, smoothing his sweatshirt, "for that you owe me one demonstration bar routine."

"Yours or mine?" Casey asked the girls.

They chose their own routine and Casey kipped to the low bar and went through the Class III compulsory routine that the girls were competing with that fall. When she dismounted, they applauded her.

Casey bowed and turned to Chip. "I'm going to work on some new things on the floor. When you're finished, I'd like to talk to you."

Chip nodded, and Casey went to the spring floor, determined to learn some of the stunts she had seen on the videos the previous night. They were harder than she had anticipated, but she stuck with it until Chip dismissed the younger team. When she saw him go into his office, Casey followed him and sat down in the overstuffed chair that faced his desk.

"It's good to see you, Casey, but I have a hunch this isn't just a social visit," Chip said, sitting down as well. He took his baseball cap and turned it around on his head. "So, the doctor is in."

Casey grinned. Chip could always raise her spirits, and he was so easy to talk to. She looked down and picked at the tear on the chair arm while she decided where to begin.

When she didn't say anything, Chip asked, "How's the team?"

"I hate it!" Casey exclaimed. "No, I don't actually hate the team. It's just . . . working with my dad . . ." She trailed off. Nothing she could say would express how she really felt about the situation.

"He's making your life miserable?" Chip suggested.

Casey grinned. "Can you tell? Chip, I was wondering. Can't I just come back here and work on Elite stuff?" She looked at him eagerly.

Chip shook his head. "No, Casey, you can't come back until after the high school season is over." He paused. "Except for extra sessions like today."

"You don't want me back?" Casey couldn't believe that.

"No, it's not that. I miss having you here—all three of you. It's not the same without you clowning around." Chip tipped back in his desk chair. "But I can't get between you and your father. He's my friend, too, and we've talked about you."

"He called you?" Casey felt empty, as if Chip had let her down. She had hoped that he'd be her go-between, and instead they had teamed up against her.

"He's worried about you—says you're not doing your best. He's afraid it will hurt your chances in the Elite meet," Chip said.

"Yeah, sure. All he does is bite my head off—for everything!" Casey complained.

"Are you sure you aren't blowing it out of proportion?"

Casey felt all her muscles tighten as tears of frustration formed in the corners of her eyes. "Chip, you should see him at practice. He doesn't yell at anyone else the way he yells at me."

"Maybe it's because he cares the most about you," Chip suggested.

"He sure doesn't act like it." Casey nervously picked at the hole in the chair again.

"Give him a chance."

Casey jumped to her feet and went to look out the window. "Everybody tells me to give him a chance. But does he give *me* a chance? No." She took a deep breath. "Chip, this past month has been torture. I want to quit the team."

Chip sat watching Casey for a minute or two. "Do you really want that?" he finally asked. "You did well at the first meet, and you bring a lot to your team. Don't you think quitting is the easy way out?"

She stared out the window, watching two little girls chase each other as they waited for a ride home. She remembered doing the same thing herself the day Jo transferred to the gym from the YWCA. That was so long ago, and yet even then she had dreamed of being the best. Her father had wanted the same thing for her. Who would have thought they would end up on opposite sides?

She turned back to Chip, who was patiently waiting for her answer. His usual smile was gone, and she couldn't read his expression. Actually, she'd be glad to get away from the team. With the exception of Monica and Jo, the other girls hadn't treated her very well. She remembered the taunts about being the coach's daughter and the gossip about her being stuck up. But even as she went over these excuses, she knew Chip was right. "I'm not sure," she finally answered. "I guess I should try again."

Chip grinned at her. "That's my girl. I knew you couldn't quit."

"I'll stay for a while, but I'm not promising anything." She forced herself to return his smile.

"That's good enough for me." He swung his feet off the desk and got up. "Well, I'm ready for lunch. You want to work any longer?"

"No." Casey got to her feet. "Monica and Jo and I are going to get our costumes ready to wear to school Monday. Halloween is a dress-up day."

"Aha! I suggest you go as three devils." He came around the desk and put his arm across Casey's shoulders. "Remember, Bear has a dream for you. *He* didn't make it all the way to the Olympics. He thinks that you have a chance. Now get out of here."

Early Monday morning Casey arrived at Jo's house with a grocery bag full of sweats for her costume. This morning the Mallorys' kitchen was bustling as Jo's mom helped a small tow-headed boy adjust his clown ruffle while a pirate stood by with makeup in his hand. Jo pinned a tiara on her youngest sister, who fidgeted in a pink tutu and ballet slippers. One of six children, Jo was used to helping get everyone off to school.

"I can handle it now," Mrs. Mallory said. "You go get ready."

Jo hugged her sister. "Okay, princess. You're all set."

Casey followed Jo upstairs and they started to transform themselves into Smurfs. Monica burst into Jo's room a few minutes later. "I got the blue makeup!" she announced.

"Great! Let's hurry. We don't have much time." Casey stepped into her white sweat pants and pulled the hooded white sweatshirt over her head as the others did the same.

"Here are the blue shirts." Jo handed each of her friends a royal blue sweatshirt to wear over the white one.

Monica opened up the package of makeup. "Here goes," she said as she dabbed the bright blue on her face.

When they'd finished, they surveyed themselves in the mirror. Satisfied with their appearance, they gathered up their books. "We're out of here!" Jo said.

When they reached school, Casey said good-bye to her friends and headed for the art room. Brett was waiting for her outside the door. She gasped. He was wearing the skeleton T-shirt he had made.

A look of disappointment flickered across his brightly painted face when he saw her Smurf costume. "Hi, Casey. I thought maybe you'd wear your shirt, too."

"Oh, Brett, I'm sorry. I'd made plans with Monica and Jo to do this today. I would have worn yours to the dance, though, for sure." She paused. "So how was it?"

"The dance? Oh, I didn't go." He opened the door for her. "How were the tapes?"

"They were terrific. The Romanian girl had a fantastic mount on the beam, and some of the tumbling runs were unbelievable. I went back to the Flyaway Gym Saturday morning to—" She stopped. Here she was, running on about the tapes, when he'd missed the dance because of her. "Never mind. They were okay, but I would have rather gone out with you."

Brett grinned. "Yes, but would you be the best gymnast in the whole state if you had? It sounds like the videos were something you shouldn't have missed. Don't worry—there'll be other dances."

Other dances? Then there was still hope, Casey told herself. A little, anyway.

That afternoon, standing on the balance beam, Casey looked around the gym. So far, workout had been a total disaster. She was trying *too* hard to do well. Bear noticed every mistake she made, and the harder she tried to correct her errors, the worse she got. She had already fallen off the beam three times—twice in one routine! She shook her head and got ready to begin again.

Stretching high, she soared over the beam in a stag leap with her front knee bent. Landing lightly, she finished her first pass with a full turn, dropping into a sitting position straddling the beam. Supporting her body with her hands, she slowly pushed herself up into a handstand. Finally, she dismounted with an aerial somersault.

It's about time I finished without falling off, Casey thought. She sneaked a peek at her dad but was disappointed when she saw he had his back to her. *You might know he wouldn't notice the one time I do something right!* She sighed and climbed back on the beam to do it again.

As she reached the handstand, Casey tightened her muscles, and hand over hand she turned her body in a circle. Completing her turn, she felt herself losing control. Before she could regain her balance, she tumbled to the mat and crashed onto it with a loud "smack."

"For gosh sakes, Casey! Concentrate!" Bear yelled. He hurried over to the beam. "Are you hurt?"

"I just . . . lost my breath," she answered, gulping in some air. Had she actually heard some concern in his voice? she wondered.

"That's not all you lost," he snapped, offering her his hand.

Ignoring him, Casey struggled to her feet by herself.

"Try not to scare me like that." He looked at her and shook his head. "What's wrong with you these past weeks? Your gymnastics are going to . . . oh, never mind. Take a few minutes to collect yourself, and then do it again." Abruptly, he turned and strode back to the parallel bars.

Casey stared after him. *Scare him?* she thought. *Is that all he cares about? That and his precious team.* At first, she'd thought he was worried about her, but it was pretty obvious that he just didn't want to be inconvenienced.

Angry, she jumped back up and started again. Propelled by fury, she threw herself into her back handspring. Before she was halfway through the routine, though, she had fallen off the beam three times. That only made her attack it harder. By the final move, before her dismount, she crashed to the floor again.

This time she didn't even bother to get back on the beam. It was no use. She couldn't do anything right. She decided to move on to the vault.

"Benson!" Bear yelled.

She sighed. What did he want now? "Yes, *Coach*?" she answered.

"Go home! Take the afternoon off!" Bear shouted across the room. "You're going to kill yourself!"

Astonished, Casey stared at her dad. He was actually sending her home! And worse, everyone in the gym knew that she had been dismissed. Mortified and humiliated, she fled from the room.

This was the last straw! She didn't care what Chip or anyone else said! There was no way she could stay on the team and work with her dad any longer. She'd finish up this week and then she'd quit after the meet with Arnold High.

Maybe then her life would get back to normal.

Chapter 12

★ ★ ★ ★ ★ ★ ★ ★ ★ ★

WEDNESDAY morning Casey looked around the art room. It was hard to believe that the class she had dreaded the most had turned out to be her favorite—although art certainly had nothing to do with it.

When Casey set her books down on the table she shared with Brett, he asked, "Do you like football?"

Casey shrugged. "I don't know."

"What?" Brett stared at her as his paintbrush dripped bright red paint onto the paper in front of him.

"I really don't. I've never even been to a game," Casey admitted.

Brett gave her a look of total disbelief. "But Tom's the star! The whole school's talking about him."

"Everyone but me." She looked down at the puddle design he was making while they talked.

"Haven't you ever gone to see him?" Brett asked.

Casey took a sketch pad off the shelf behind her and sat down. "I've always had gymnastics. And the games my dad and brother watched on TV just seemed confusing." She took a pencil out of her knapsack and started drawing the maple tree in their backyard.

"I still can't believe it," Brett said, shaking his head.

"Brett, you just don't understand. If you want to be a good gymnast, you have to work at it constantly. That means no clubs, no games ... no dances. Total dedication."

"Do you think it's worth it?"

Casey waited a minute before answering. She wasn't sure anymore. "I've grown up on it, so I've always believed it. I guess in a way I still do. It's hard to give up that dream," she said softly.

Brett looked puzzled. "Who's giving up?"

"No one—yet. It's just that I've been thinking about quitting lately. Not gymnastics, but the Fairfield team."

Finally noticing his dripping paint, Brett groaned and started mopping up the mess. Casey went back to sketching, trying to ignore the unhappy feeling she got whenever she thought about gymnastics.

After a minute of silence Brett said, "Why don't you come to the game with me tomorrow night?" He hesitated. "It would be good for you."

Casey knew she should be thrilled by the invitation. After the Halloween dance disaster, she had given up his ever asking her out again. But her dad would be furious with her if she left practice early for a football game. "I don't know. It would mean skipping practice, and we have a meet coming up. My dad would have a fit."

"Why don't you just say you feel sick? Pretend you pulled a muscle or something," Brett suggested.

"You don't call in sick for workout. Especially not when your dad is the coach."

"Please, Casey? It'll be fun, I promise."

She looked into his pleading eyes. How could she turn Brett down again? But how could she skip practice? Casey thought about it for a minute or two. Well, why not? If her father hadn't been treating her so badly, she would never even consider missing workout. And if he kicked her off the team because of it, her problem would be solved. She could go back to Chip and start training for the Elite Championships again.

"You know what, Brett? I will go with you," Casey said. "I don't care what my father thinks. I'll find a way to get out of practice."

His wide grin was all the thanks she needed.

Friday afternoon Casey asked Jo to tell her dad she felt sick and was going home. That seemed easy enough, but as she neared their two-story brick house, her steps slowed. Convincing her mom that she was really sick would take some doing.

She stopped on the front sidewalk and gazed up at the big house with its white trim. She'd lived there all her life, and there had been so many happy times within its walls. Casey hated to go inside feeling so guilty.

Nothing like this had ever happened before; gymnastics had always been the highlight of her life. Now the sport was ruining everything. Suddenly Casey wished her sister were home from college so she could talk it over with her. Barbara would know what to do.

Slowly, Casey forced herself to open the door. Luck was on her side; her mother was on the phone in the kitchen, and Casey could sneak upstairs without explaining too much. She called a weak greeting to her mom.

"Casey? Is that you?" Mrs. Benson asked, obviously surprised as she leaned out from the kitchen. She put her hand over the phone and pulled the long cord through the door. "What's wrong? Why aren't you at the gym?"

"I feel awful. I've got a really bad headache." She put her hand to her forehead and hoped she looked pale. "I'm going to lie down."

Climbing the stairs, Casey realized that she hadn't brought any books home. Shrugging, she undressed and put on her skeleton T-shirt. She threw back the covers on her bed and climbed in. As an afterthought she hopped up and placed the aspirin bottle on her dresser, leaving off the lid to make it look as if she had just taken a few.

Back in bed, she pulled up the rose print bedspread under her chin. When the gymnastics posters on her closet door caught her eye, she turned away. She didn't want to face gymnastics today in any form.

A few minutes later she heard a soft knock, and then her mother tiptoed into the room. "Casey," she whispered. "Are you asleep?"

"Um," Casey moaned.

"What would give you a headache?" Mrs. Benson probed. "Have you had any problems at school? Your dad says you're not doing your best at gymnastics. Is it tough being at such a big school?"

Casey wanted to say, *It's not the school, it's the coach!* But this was not the time to get into that argument. Instead, she said, "Must be the big English report. It's due soon and I'm kinda nervous about it."

"Well, don't worry. You probably just need some sleep. I see you already took some aspirin." Mrs. Benson screwed the lid back on the bottle. "I'll check on you later."

After her mother left, Casey felt a terrible wave of guilt. She hated being dishonest. What if her mom found out she was lying? She couldn't believe it had been so easy. Maybe her mother knew she was faking—maybe she would understand what everyone else hadn't, that she needed a break from her dad. Casey wondered what Monica and Jo would think if they knew what she was doing. She hadn't dared confide in them; she couldn't take any chances if she wanted to go to the game.

When she awoke, the house was quiet, and it had started to get dark. Reaching for her alarm clock, Casey saw it was six-fifteen. She was supposed to meet Brett outside school at seven. She leapt out of bed and took a shower in record time. She brushed her tangle of curls, glad for once that she didn't have to do anything more with her hair. Then she put on some lip gloss and a tiny bit of blush.

Standing in front of the closet, Casey realized she didn't even know what people wore to football games. Since it would be cold, she chose her jeans and a cream-colored cable knit sweater. Fishing her brown leather ankle boots out from under the bed, she headed downstairs. In the kitchen she found a note from her mother.

Casey,
   I left for the game. You were sleeping so soundly, I didn't want to wake you. If you're hungry, there's dinner in the fridge.
                                        Love, Mom

Casey didn't even bother to warm up the lasagna she pulled from the refrigerator. She devoured a few bites of the cold pasta, then quickly threw on her hat, gloves, and tan jacket as she ran out the door.

Outside, she caught her breath as the crisp, cold air stung her nose. She pulled her hat down over her ears. It was going to be a cold night.

Brett was standing under a light outside the front of the school, jumping up and down to keep warm. Under his arm he held a folded blanket. When he saw Casey, he waved and walked up to meet her. "Any problems getting out?" he asked.

"No, it was almost *too* easy," she answered, thinking how it had all fallen into place. "But we have to keep an eye out for both my parents. My mom's already here—she goes to every game."

Brett took her arm and steered her in the direction of the stadium behind the school. "Doesn't your dad have practice?"

"Yeah, but he always comes over for the last part. And if he finds me here instead of home in bed . . ." She drew her finger across her throat.

"We'll look for them, but we're going to sit in the student section. They'll never see you." Brett said hello to a group of boys who came up behind them.

As they neared the stadium, they were joined by crowds of students carrying blankets, seat cushions, and blue and gold pom-poms on wood sticks. Casey felt swept along as they funneled through the ticket gate. "I had no idea how many came to these games," she said.

"I told you it would be fun." Brett smiled at her and took her hand.

Casey tensed. There was no way Brett wouldn't notice how rough her palms were.

He ran his thumb over the calluses. "I guess those are the hazards of a dangerous occupation," he said, still grinning.

"Yeah," Casey agreed, relieved that he didn't seem to mind. "It goes with gymnastics."

After they climbed up the bleachers and found a place to sit, Brett spread out the blanket for them. When he sat down close to her, Casey decided the game was worth it, just to be so near him. Reluctantly, she stood up for the kickoff with everyone else.

Casey watched the game, bewildered at first, but as Brett explained it, she eventually figured out what was happening on the field. When Tom scored a touchdown in the second quarter, she found herself screaming and pounding Brett on the arm.

"Hey! That's not a punching bag!" He grimaced in mock pain.

Casey patted his arm. She wanted to offer to kiss it and make it all better. But just thinking that made Casey's face turn red! She looked away and pretended to be absorbed in people-watching.

At halftime, Brett asked her if she wanted to go down and walk around. Casey shook her head. "It's safer up here. I don't want to take any chances." Though her mother was in the parents' section on the other end, she felt more secure staying where she was, surrounded by cheering students.

During the second half, Tom scored two more touchdowns, and for the first time Casey began to see why everyone was so excited about her brother. Out on the field he was terrific. It was too bad she wouldn't be able to tell him what a great game he had played.

Casey spotted her father when he arrived near the end of the game to stand at the fence behind the end zone. She recognized the gold shirt and royal blue booster jacket he wore to all the games.

Oddly, seeing him there put Casey at ease. It was like holding on to the queen of spades in a game of hearts—at last you knew where the most dangerous card was.

As the fourth quarter wound down, Fairfield was leading by three touchdowns, and Brett suggested that they leave a few minutes early. "That way we can make sure we beat your folks home."

"It should be okay." Casey wound her scarf tighter around her neck. "They have a group of football boosters they always get together with after the game."

"Well, let's not blow it now." Brett folded up the blanket and they inched their way down the bleachers. Casey crouched down so that she'd be hidden by the crowd. Sometimes being five feet one inch was great!

"We didn't get as quick a start as I thought," Brett said nervously. He quickly steered her toward the school parking lot.

Suddenly they heard voices, and Casey spun around. The football team was walking behind them on their way to the locker room. Casey spotted Tom instantly, and at the exact same moment he looked up.

Tom stopped walking and stared at her. "Casey?" he mouthed silently.

She saw his expression of surprise, but when he started toward her, she grabbed Brett's hand and started running in the opposite direction.

She was dead. Tom would tell their parents, and then she'd be in deep trouble. Even holding hands with Brett couldn't erase the sense of dread that hung over her. Her father would probably kick her off the team—or at least keep her out of the next meet. Even though she had mixed feelings about the team, she didn't want that to happen.

She had probably blown her future—for one night. For a stupid football game, as her father would say.

Chapter 13

★ ★ ★ ★ ★ ★ ★ ★ ★ ★

ALL weekend Casey waited for the bombshell to drop. Tom had to have told her parents he'd seen her at the game. So why didn't they just yell at her and get it over with?

Sunday evening she decided to go to bed early. Upstairs, she found Tom sprawled on the floor in the hallway, on the phone as usual. She headed for her room, but stopped when he mentioned her name. Retracing her steps, she went back toward him as he hung up the phone. "What did you say?" she asked.

"I said, 'Hi, Casey!' "

He seemed excited, she thought, and *very* friendly. Maybe he was so happy because he had snitched on her. "Hi, yourself. What's up?"

Tom rolled over on his stomach. "I was just wondering how you got out of gymnastics Friday night."

"Since Dad hasn't blown up, does that mean you didn't tell him I was at the game?" Casey asked. She waited for his answer, and wondered what price she'd have to pay for his silence.

"Why would I tell him?" Tom replied.

"I thought you'd be glad to get me in trouble."

"You're paranoid. I'm not out to get you, little sister." He emphasized the last words.

Casey crossed her arms on her chest and looked at him. "Since when?"

Tom shrugged. He rested his head on his arms and closed his eyes. "I'm not. But if you're so sure I am, have it your way."

Casey wasn't sure what to say. Tom had done her a huge favor, and here she was accusing him of being a jerk. "Look, I'm sorry," she finally said. "Thanks for not telling them. Dad would have grounded me for life. And I did enjoy the game." She dropped into the bean bag chair.

"Hey!" He hoisted himself up into a sitting position. "That's the first game you've seen me play, isn't it?"

Casey nodded. "And I hate to admit it, but you were good—incredibly good. I had a great time."

Tom laughed. "I'm sure that guy you were with had a lot more to do with that than my playing ability."

Casey giggled. "Well, maybe a little of both."

"Who's the guy?" he asked.

Oh, no, she thought. *Don't tell me he's going to play the concerned-big-brother bit.* "His name is Brett Kelly. He's in my art class."

"You like him, don't you? I can tell!"

Embarrassed, Casey looked away. "Never mind!"

"Okay." Tom leaned against the wall. "What's the story with you and Dad at gymnastics? He still bugging you?"

Casey nodded. "He's never going to let up." She took a deep breath. "I'm thinking of quitting the team."

"Whoa! This is serious." He grimaced. "Do you have any idea how Dad will react?"

Casey gave him a sheepish smile. "Yeah, that's why I haven't told him yet."

When the phone rang, Tom reached over to pick it up from the floor. Casey yawned and decided to go to bed. No doubt it was a girl on the line, and Tom would talk forever.

As she walked into her room and shut the door, Casey thought about their conversation. She still wasn't sure she trusted her older brother. He certainly *seemed* sincere, though. And he hadn't called her Cheetah in a long time. Maybe he was growing up, too.

Monday, in algebra, Casey was tapping her pencil against the desk while she waited for the bell to ring. Instead, the buzzer on her teacher's interoffice phone rang. Mrs. Knox listened a minute and then she hung up and called Casey to her desk. *Now what?* Casey thought as she gathered up her books.

"You're wanted in Coach Benson's office," Mrs. Knox informed her.

A wave of panic hit her. *He knows! Tom told him after all.* Now she would have to face him, and the whole story would come out in the open.

As she walked down the hall with her pass clutched tightly in one hand, Casey's steps grew heavier. Why did she feel as if she were going to her execution? She wished the bell would ring so she could tell him she had to go to her next class. But she knew he'd never buy that. If she didn't talk to him now, he would just get angrier with her.

As she stood outside his door, Casey realized she

was shaking. Taking a deep breath, she opened the door. *Here goes nothing,* she thought.

Coach Benson stood looking out the window. When he heard the door, he turned around and gave her an icy-cold look.

If he's trying to make me feel terrible, he's doing a great job, Casey said to herself.

Finally, he spoke. "So, now football is more important than gymnastics. First dances, and now the game."

Casey didn't even try to defend herself. It was no use.

"What happened to your dream of being the best?" he continued softly, and Casey wondered if it was a hurt expression she saw in his eyes. No, it couldn't be. Not the way he had been acting.

She sat down in the chair opposite his desk. Ignoring his question, she asked, "Did Tom tell you?"

"Tom?" Bear practically shouted. "You mean he knew you were there?"

Uh-oh. Now she had Tom in trouble, too. "He saw me after the game. He was so psyched about the win, he probably didn't realize that I was supposed to be at practice," she improvised, hoping it would get Tom off the hook.

"Half the teachers at this school saw you there, Casey. You can't go to a football game and not be seen."

Casey let out a long sigh. "I guess you're right."

"You guess?" Bear's face turned red with emotion. "What kind of example are you setting for the rest of the team? My own daughter skipping practice."

"That seems to be the problem—me being your daughter," Casey pointed out.

"Daughter or not, you don't skip practice!" he admonished her.

Casey shifted in her seat. "It was only one time," she argued.

"One time is too often!" he yelled. "I'm trying to build a team, trying to win League! And if you can't follow the rules, you're off the team."

Casey jumped to her feet. "Well, if you want to kick me off the team, it's fine with me! Now you won't have anyone to yell at!" She raced for the door, determined not to let him see the tears in her eyes.

"Casey, wait! I didn't kick you off the—" Bear called after her as she ran out of the office.

But Casey kept running down the hall, away from him and his accusations. On her way to her locker she saw Tom. He grinned and started to give a Tarzan yell but caught himself in time. "Hey, Casey! What's up?"

"Dad kicked me off the team, that's what's up!" She hurried past him, eager to get away from school. There was no way she could stick around, not after what had happened.

She couldn't face the rest of the team—not even Monica and Jo, her best friends. But there they were, standing next to her locker, waiting to go to lunch with her. She groaned. She just wanted to go home, but going home meant seeing her dad, too. If only she could run away somewhere else . . .

"I'm going home!" Casey said, grabbing her coat from her locker.

"What's wrong?" Monica asked, exchanging a worried glance with Jo.

"You've got another class! Aren't you going to

science? And what about workout?" Jo reminded her. She'd never seen Casey so angry before.

"Why does he always have to yell at me," Casey spat out. She threw her books in her locker and slammed the door.

"Come on, Casey," Jo pleaded. "I don't know what just happened, but you can't let your dad get to you. He'll calm down soon, I'm sure."

Casey looked at her best friends. "You just don't understand! I can't take it anymore!"

Speechless, Jo stared at Casey. She shifted her books in her arms and finally looked at Monica for help.

"Casey, we know your dad is being hard on you," Monica said sympathetically. "But it's just because you're his daughter."

Casey glowered at Monica and turned back to click her combination lock shut. "Yeah, well, I'm sick of being his daughter."

Jo grabbed Casey's arm. "We want to help you. What can we do?"

"It's too late," Casey snapped, and then lowered her voice, her eyes filling with tears. "I'm quitting the team."

"You can't!" Jo gasped.

Casey didn't answer. She took off down the hall without saying good-bye.

Monica and Jo stared after her. "Do you think she means it?" Monica whispered.

"I don't know." Jo shook her head. "I've never seen her so upset . . . or so down on gymnastics."

"We've got to stop her," Monica said. "We can't let her quit."

"I know. We'll have to think of something." Jo stared down the empty hall, frustrated that she couldn't help. She and Casey had been together for so long—and gymnastics had been their whole lives. If Casey hadn't been there—if she hadn't been the person to beat, Jo knew she would have never been as good as she now was. If she succeeded in getting a scholarship to college, it would be because of Casey. "Monica, what are we going to do!" she cried.

"We've got to make Casey think she's important to the team," Monica decided.

"Yeah, but how?" Jo asked.

"I don't know. But we'll think of something."

Silently, the girls headed for class, each lost in her own thoughts. Jo clutched her books to her chest and occasionally reached up to wipe away a tear.

Finally, Monica spoke. "Her confidence is shot. Her dad's made her think she's no good. That's the problem. She needs someone besides *us* telling her that she's a great gymnast."

"Hey, wait a minute! I've got an idea," Jo said. "There's a meet this week, right?"

"On Thursday," Monica answered. "So what? Doing well in the first one didn't seem to help Casey and her dad get along any better."

"I know. But I'm not talking about the judges' scores. Listen, the first thing we have to do is . . ." Jo outlined her plan as they walked to the cafeteria. Monica seemed equally excited by it. *Now, if only Casey likes it!* Jo thought.

Casey covered the distance to her house in record time. When she saw her mom's car in the drive, she stopped. She didn't want to talk to anyone right now. She had to escape to her room.

Yanking open the front door, she took the stairs two at a time and raced into her bedroom. Jamming the lock shut, she dumped her books on her desk. She threw herself on the bed and pulled the covers over her head.

From under the comforter she could hear her mother's footsteps coming down the hallway. Casey braced herself for the questions.

"Casey? Casey, what's wrong, honey?" Mrs. Benson tried to open the door.

"Ask Dad!" Casey snapped from under the covers.

The doorknob stopped rattling. "Do you want to talk?"

"No! Just leave me alone!"

Mrs. Benson paused for a minute. "If you change your mind, call me. Or come down and I'll make some hot chocolate."

When Casey heard her mother return to the kitchen, she pulled the bedspread off her face. Mom's solution to every problem was hot chocolate. But this was something that wouldn't go away with love and a hot drink. A tear ran down her face and fell onto her pillow. She hadn't realized how horrible and lonely she would feel once she was off the team. *Dad didn't actually say I was off now,* she thought, *only I would be if I broke the rules again.* Still, she'd been going to quit anyway. She hadn't actually said she was quitting, but she had no other choice now.

She should be happy—no more practices, no more having Dad yell at her, no more missing dances and school activities.

Then why did she feel so awful?

When she was called for dinner, Casey told her mother she wasn't hungry. There was no way she was going to eat at the same table with her father.

Let them talk about her all they wanted. She didn't care.

Finally, Casey's growling stomach got the best of her. She tiptoed down to the kitchen and made herself a peanut butter sandwich and poured some milk into a glass. On her way back upstairs she heard Tom talking to her dad in his study. She stopped abruptly when they mentioned her name.

"Casey's acting sort of strange these days," Tom said. "Is she doing okay on the gymnastics team?"

"She's not even trying!" Bear's voice boomed out, making Casey jump.

"She told me you kicked her off the team today."

A fist slammed the desk. "I did not kick her off the team." He lowered his voice a notch. "But she must have thought I did because she wasn't at practice today and now she's hiding out in her room." Bear sighed. "I told her I *might* kick her off if she broke the rules again—by going to another football game, for instance."

"Have you ever thought that maybe you're being too hard on her?" Tom asked softly.

Surprised that her brother would come to her defense, Casey stepped back from the door. She listened to her dad's footsteps, and she could picture him pacing back and forth in front of the fireplace. She wondered if Tom would tell him she had been thinking of quitting lately.

"All this training, and she's throwing it all away," Bear said in a sad voice.

"Admit it, Dad. You need her to win League and State this year," Tom challenged.

"Yes, the team does need her. I'll admit that."

Casey felt a pang of remorse. Her father was right. If Fairfield was going to beat Arnold High, they would need her to perform at her best. How could she abandon them?

"Maybe you should ease up a little, Dad," Tom suggested. "She might work better if you left her alone during practice, for once."

Casey heard him slam his fist down on the desk again. "She's a gymnast! She's used to working under pressure. Besides, a coach just doesn't stand by and keep quiet. I'm paid to *coach* the team, to make each girl the best she can be."

"Okay, forget it!" Tom stormed out of the room and Casey barely slipped behind the door before he raced past. Taking a deep breath, she froze in place until she heard Bear sit down in his squeaky desk chair again.

When the coast was clear, she started to leave. But just as she stepped out from the door, she heard her mother call, "What's going on in there?"

Casey jumped back behind the door. *This place is as busy as O'Hare Airport*, she thought. From the slit near the hinges, Casey saw her mother walk into the den from the kitchen. Mrs. Benson dried her hands on the short apron Casey had made for her in seventh-grade sewing class. "Bear? What's all the ruckus?" she asked.

From her hiding place Casey heard Bear sigh and tip back in his chair. "It seems I'm number one on both Tom's and Casey's hit list."

"I can understand how *she* feels, but what about Tom?" Mrs. Benson inquired.

"Tom was defending her. He thinks that I'm being too hard on her." He sighed loudly.

"So I've heard."

Bear's chair squeaked to an upright position. "You're in on it, too? Donna, she's not even trying to be the best. My own daughter, whom I've taught everything I know."

"Honey, I think her being your daughter is the problem," Mrs. Benson put in. "What's been going on at the gym?"

"I've bent over backward to treat her like the others—no special favors. She and those buddies of hers are better than any of the others. I figured the older girls would hold that against them, so I wanted to show them I wouldn't play favorites. Maybe . . . maybe I have been a little hard . . ." Bear's voice trailed off.

"And just maybe that's why she's stopped try-ing." Mrs. Benson said softly.

A little hard? Casey thought. *He thinks that's just a little?* But she could see that her father thought he was doing the right thing. He just had a funny way of going about it.

Hearing her dad talk about the team had made Casey realize that she couldn't let them down, not now. She'd have to stick it out for the rest of the season.

Then next year, well, she'd see.

Chapter 14

★ ★ ★ ★ ★ ★ ★ ★ ★ ★

AT noon in the cafeteria on Thursday Casey watched as Monica and Jo rushed through their lunches. "What's the big hurry? You two look like you're having a race."

"Sorry, Casey." Jo shoved her tray away and stood up. "We've got to hit the library."

"Mr. Dodge assigned us a take-home quiz in history, and we have to look up some books on the American Revolution."

Jo smiled. "Look, we'll see you at the gym this afternoon. We're going to kill Arnold!"

"Yeah, right," Casey mumbled halfheartedly.

Casey watched her friends walk away. After they'd put their trays on the conveyor belt to the kitchen, they burst out laughing. Jo looked back and waved as they walked out of the cafeteria. *Why do I get the feeling they're talking about me?* Casey wondered.

"What are you doing eating alone?" Jill suddenly slid into Jo's empty chair.

Casey shrugged. "Jo and Monica had to go to the library." She knew she shouldn't be talking to

131

Jill, but she felt so lonely that a friendly face was welcome—even if Jill was a fake friend.

"You didn't want to go, too?" Jill asked.

"They didn't ask me to." It was almost as if they didn't want her to come, Casey thought. The last few days Monica and Jo had spent all their time together, and Casey was feeling left out. It was as if her friends were mad at her for skipping workout that Monday. She shouldn't have told them she was thinking about quitting the team. They were obviously holding it against her.

Jill's eyes sparkled as she leaned across the table. "Did you hear the good news? Tom asked me out!"

"Yeah, I heard," Casey said almost glumly. She knew she ought to act more excited about it, but she wasn't thrilled that Ginny's prediction had come true. Jill had used her to get to Tom. Now that she had a date with him, Jill wouldn't need Casey anymore.

Jill grinned. "You could at least *try* to look pleased. What's the matter? Don't you want me to go out with him?"

"It's not that." Casey sighed and poked at her leftover vanilla pudding. "I'm just worried that it'll ruin our friendship."

"Don't be silly!" Jill cried. "It'll only make it better. We'll see even more of each other now."

"That's not what Ginny said," Casey blurted out.

"Oh, really? What *did* Ginny say?"

Casey let out a long breath and wished she hadn't mentioned it. "That you wanted to be friends with me only to get to Tom."

"That's ridiculous! Casey, have you ever noticed that when we do things together, we laugh a lot? I like that. You're a great friend!"

Casey thought back to the times they had spent together. Remembering their lurching jeep ride to the mall, she smiled. "I guess we do."

"Come on, sourpuss. I'll walk you to your locker." She stood up and picked up her tray. "Everything is going to be fine. Don't worry." She squeezed Casey's arm affectionately. "So, are you going to win that beam routine today, or what?"

As Casey headed for the gym that afternoon, she told herself that she only had to get through today's dual meet—then she could put all of the problems behind her. This was an important meet. Arnold High's team included a number of girls from the Aerial Gym Club, which was an excellent private club. She'd give it her best shot this afternoon, and if it didn't work out, she would go back to Flyaway and start preparing for the Elite Championship in earnest.

Workouts *had* been easier that week. When she'd walked into gym on Tuesday afternoon, Bear had stood across the gym watching her, his hands on his hips. Finally, with a curt nod, he'd turned his back and begun adjusting the uneven bars. Throughout practice Casey found herself ignored by her dad, but she'd been delighted by his silence. Maybe some good had come out of his talking to her mother and Tom.

Now, as she walked into the locker room, Casey sighed. The ordeal was almost over.

Monica and Jo were nowhere in sight, and Casey couldn't help wondering what was going on with them. Usually they all waited for one another at their lockers to go to the gym. Casey felt left out, and she missed the nervous laughter the three of them always shared before a big meet. Maybe once she left the team Jo and Monica wouldn't want to be her friends at all.

After dressing quickly, Casey ran into the gym to warm up. Suddenly she stopped. The bleachers were full of kids, all talking and laughing, some of them holding blue and gold helium balloons. High on the wall a large paper banner read, "Go Fairfield Gymnastics!"

Casey couldn't believe her eyes. In the past, her dad had done everything but bribe his students to come to the meets, and now the gym was spilling over with fans. It looked as if the whole student body had arrived. She studied the crowd. It wasn't *all* the school—just a lot of freshmen and sophomores.

Jill followed her out of the locker room. "What's going on?" she asked, looking around in amazement.

"Beats me," Casey answered. "But it's kind of exciting!"

"I can hardly believe this," Jill said. "I've never seen so many people at a gymnastics meet."

"Me either." Casey shook her head. "Well, let's give them a show."

On the vault Casey did a few handsprings, and then worked up to the harder Tsukahara. When she landed she received some applause from the bleachers. She smiled. Maybe they thought the meet had already started.

On the way to the beam she glanced up at the crowd, which was still growing. She heard someone calling her name.

"Casey!" Brett stood waving from the top of the bleachers. He wore a bright gold T-shirt with blue letters spelling I FLIP FOR GYMNASTICS. In his hand he held a large balloon with Casey's name on it. Five other boys wearing matching shirts sat next to him.

Casey felt her face turn pink. She was happy to see Brett, but a little embarrassed by all the attention. Was he behind all the fanfare? she asked herself.

She waved back and went to the beam to finish warming up. She took her turn, stopping before her dismount to repeat the more difficult parts. The students in the stands continued to cheer loudly. It was the most fun Casey had had in a long time— it felt exhilarating to have so many people watch her. She sailed off the end of the beam in a double twist, nailed her landing, and then went to look for Monica and Jo.

She found them whispering together, standing at the back of the line for the uneven bars. When she walked up, they stopped abruptly and stood grinning at her.

"What do you think of all this?" Jo asked, nudging Casey.

Glancing at the crowd over her shoulder, Casey said, "It's fantastic! But what are they all doing here? Is it a P.E. assignment?" she joked.

"I guess they just walked in," Monica said.

"No way. Someone had to have organized this— it wouldn't just happen." Casey examined her friends' faces. They were grinning as if they knew something she didn't. "Did you guys have anything to do with this?" she asked.

"*Us?*" Monica and Jo exclaimed in unison.

"Maybe it was Brett," Monica suggested.

Casey looked at Brett again. He was leaning casually against the wall at the top of the bleachers. "Why would he do all this?"

"Maybe he's your number one fan." Jo slipped her arm around Casey's waist. "Besides us, that is."

"Don't I wish!" Casey joked, but secretly she felt a warm flush of pleasure that Brett was in the audience with all those people—and the shirts! He must have silk-screened them just as he had for the other clubs. It felt great to have his support.

Suddenly she thought of her dad. What would he think of all this? What if he hated it? She spotted him talking to a group of freshmen who were sitting on the lowest bleachers. He was smiling. Casey heaved a sigh of relief and resumed her warmups.

When the meet began, Coach Benson introduced Arnold High. The opposing team looked impressive in their red and white geometric-print leotards as they took their places on the chairs set up by the floor exercise, their first event.

Bear announced the names of the Fairfield team members, and the crowd cheered wildly. When Casey stepped forward, they sounded even louder. She stifled a grin and decided she'd pretend they were her own personal cheering section.

Mr. Benson paused and smiled. He shook his head as if he just couldn't believe there was so much student-body support, and then continued introducing his girls.

The Fairfield team started the meet with the vault and then went to the balance beam. Casey, again seeded last for her team in beam, watched the other gymnasts. Each time a Fairfield girl did an aerial move or finished her dismount, the crowd cheered loudly.

As Casey's turn neared, Jo leaned over to whisper, "Check this next girl out. She's supposed to be good."

The Arnold High gymnast did a great routine

and finished with an 8.8 score, which brought applause even from the biased audience. Casey winced. "She'll be hard to beat," she whispered back.

"No way!" Monica assured her. "We'll blow her away!"

"You can do it!" Jo said, her eyes dancing with excitement. "Besides, you've got the crowd with you."

Casey considered her two grinning friends, and wondered if they *did* have something to do with this crazy group today.

"Yeah, go get em!" Monica urged as Casey's name was called.

When Casey stepped into place to begin her beam routine, the students began cheering, "Yay, Casey!" She looked into the stands to see Brett's friends standing up, frantically waving their balloons. She swallowed a giggle and saluted the judge.

The judge shook her head and gave Bear a questioning look. Stepping to the front of the bleachers, he blew his whistle. The crowd grew silent quickly. "We're really glad you all turned out today, but these routines are very difficult," Bear said. He motioned to the beam. "How'd you like to do all this stuff on a board only four inches wide, with all this racket?"

"No way!" one student called out.

"Not me!" another yelled.

"So," Bear continued, "how about saving the applause and cheering for the end of each routine?"

This time the kids merely applauded to show that they agreed with him. Casey expected her father to be upset, but he chuckled as he walked back to the beam. Now, *that* was more like the dad she knew.

Casey grinned and saluted the judge again before beginning her routine. The crowd's support had produced a crazy electricity inside her, and she felt like giving the performance of her lifetime.

She punched the springboard and sprang onto the beam. She sailed through the beginning with ease. The crowd gasped when she pushed up into a handstand and started to turn her body in a full circle. She danced through the rest of her routine, completing each move with her own special flair.

When she dismounted with a double somersault and stuck her landing, the crowd roared its approval.

In the midst of the noise Casey heard Tom give his Tarzan yell. Whirling around, she saw him leaning against the bleachers in his football practice gear. He gave her a thumbs-up sign. Even his pesty yell didn't bother her this time. He had come to the meet to watch her, and suddenly that seemed like the most important thing.

Casey didn't know what was going on, but she loved it. When they put up her score, she was ecstatic. Her 9.0 was the highest so far, and she was pretty sure it would win. The cheering continued, so she stepped forward and raised her hand to the students just as she had seen Mary Lou Retton do on TV. She felt like a real star.

The crowd warmed to the other Fairfield girls, too, and the more they yelled, the better the girls scored. When the final results were in, Bear's team had walked away with the meet.

The enthusiasm in the gym was contagious, and Casey felt as if she were three feet off the ground.

Dad may not like my performance, she thought, *but everyone else thinks I'm doing just fine.*

After the awards had been handed out, many of the students stopped to congratulate Casey.

A redheaded boy from her art class approached her. "I'm sure glad Brett invited us," he said, pounding her on the back. "You were the greatest! When's the next one?"

"We have a dual meet almost every Thursday," Casey said, her mind racing. So it really *was* Brett who had organized the whole thing!

"I'll be here!" the boy called, heading for the door.

The crowd thinned out and Casey noticed some of the spectators were helping to put the equipment away. Realizing Brett hadn't come down to see her, she looked around for him. He was still sitting in the stands.

From the top row he smiled at her as she climbed up the bleachers toward him. She felt a little like the helium in his balloon—as if she might float away at any minute, she was so happy.

"You were fantastic!" he said as he tied the balloon around her wrist. When he finished he continued to hold her hand, rubbing his thumb over her callused palm. "All that work really paid off."

"I'm so excited! We beat Arnold High in spite of all those girls from the Aerial Gym Club!"

"I never had any doubts," Brett assured her.

"I'm sorry I haven't been friendly the last few days. It was just that I had all that pressure from Dad . . . and I was actually thinking of quitting," she explained.

Brett nodded. "I understand. But I hope there will be a little time for me in the future."

So he did still like her. That added the finishing

touch to the afternoon. Casey smiled up at him.
"I'm still going to be really busy. We have the rest
of the dual meets and then the League . . . and
then there's State, if we make it . . ."

He grinned. "Well, we may not have a lot of
time together, but we can at least be friends." He
put his arm around her. "Good friends."

Casey leaned her head against Brett's shoulder.
Everything was finally working out. Maybe she
couldn't go out with Brett, but she knew he would
always be there for her, cheering her on in the
background. And suddenly that was enough.

Chapter 15

★ ★ ★ ★ ★ ★ ★ ★ ★

FOR the first time since she'd started high school, Casey felt that being a gymnast was the most wonderful thing in the world.

"Did you like the cheering section we dreamed up?" Jo asked as they walked home together that evening.

"I loved it!" Casey shrieked. It was so obvious now that Monica and Jo had planned the whole thing—all the times she'd found them whispering together, and how she'd felt left out. She'd been sure that their friendship was drifting. And all along they were planning this for her!

"You guys are the greatest!" She took a deep breath of crisp November air and looked at each of her friends. "I can't believe you did all that just for me."

"We were so afraid you'd quit," Jo said.

Casey sighed. "I was close. If it hadn't been for the team and you guys, I might have. I don't know. I don't really think I would have let you down like that, though. We've been through too much together!"

"Well, anyway, you didn't, and we can stop worrying." Monica did a little dance step down the sidewalk.

Jo linked her arm through Casey's. "It was hard keeping it a secret."

"And I thought you were avoiding me. I was so envious of all the time you spent together."

"Oh, no!" Jo cried. "We never thought of that!"

"It's okay, I'm just glad it's over!" Casey said.

"Even your dad was smiling today," Monica observed. "Did you notice?"

Casey giggled. "I kept sneaking peeks at him. I couldn't believe it! He was so pleased. Do you know how hard he's worked to get kids out to the meets?"

"You should have seen his face when you came out for your first turn and the crowd went crazy." Jo let go of Casey and whirled around. "He was so surprised! It was a riot!"

Casey took a deep breath and asked sheepishly, "Did you guys notice that Brett was there? At first I thought *he* was behind the cheering section."

Jo nodded. "He sure helped a lot. He brought a bunch of sophomores and he made those wild shirts."

Monica laughed. "I was so surprised when they walked in wearing those!"

Casey smiled and hugged her books to her chest. He *had* been in on the plan. She felt a warm glow of pleasure when she thought of his balloon with her name on it.

"So what's with you two?" Monica grinned and winked at Jo.

Casey blushed. "We went to the football game last week."

"But you were sick Friday night. Weren't you?" Jo stopped as she realized what had happened. She grabbed Casey's arm. "Casey Benson, did you skip gymnastics to go to the game?"

"Without telling us!" Monica shrieked.

"I wanted to tell you." Casey smiled sheepishly at her two astonished friends. "But I didn't want Dad to find out . . . and anyway, you were always off together. I guess I've been shutting you out, too."

Monica shook her head. "I can't believe it. You actually cut workout."

"Good thing your dad didn't find out." Jo still looked as if she were in shock.

"Actually, he did. The teachers saw me and blabbed. Remember the day I left school early? That was because he chewed me out."

"Personally, I'm surprised you're still *alive*, but after today things should be fine." Monica punched Casey's arm.

"What about Brett?" Jo asked. "Are you two an item?"

"Well . . . not really. It's hard to have a boyfriend when you have gymnastics. Not that I have to tell *you* that. And when the season's over here, we'll be going back to Flyaway." Casey looked down at the sidewalk and kicked a stone. "High school is sure different from junior high. There's so much stuff to do, it's hard to keep it all balanced."

At her corner Casey gave each of her friends another hug. "Thanks for everything," she said. She promised to call each of them later that night, and then hurried home.

Bouncing up the front steps, she spun around. It had been such a wonderful day!

She deposited her books on the stairway, hung up her coat, and practically flew into the kitchen. "Mom! Are you home?" she called.

"We're here!" Mrs. Benson answered as she came in from the living room.

"Wasn't it just the greatest?" Casey did a double pirouette in the middle of the kitchen. "It was so exciting! I loved every—" Suddenly she stopped, and her smile faded. Her dad had come in behind her mom.

"I agree one hundred percent," he said. "I don't know how you convinced so many kids to come out, but you're right. It *was* exciting."

Casey felt her shoulders relax. She had been worried about his reaction. Even though he'd *seemed* happy about the meet, she hadn't been sure how he really felt. "Oh, but Dad, it wasn't me. Monica and Jo did it!"

"Well, whoever did it—it worked. The whole team came alive. I haven't seen such scores in a long time." He paused and looked at Casey. "You, too, sugar. Nice meet."

Was that an apology? Casey wondered. She wasn't sure she could forgive him quite that easily. "Thanks," she murmured.

Bear rubbed his hands together and peered into the pot on the stove. "That smells terrific! When do we eat?"

"If Casey will put the plates on the table, we're ready. Tom's still at football practice." Mrs. Benson stirred the stew and then added, "It was nice of Tom to stop by the meet, wasn't it?"

"It was great, but what did you bribe him with?" Casey teased.

"Not one penny! He said since you'd come to his game . . ."

Bear cleared his throat loudly, then smiled.

"He wanted to see you in action," Mrs. Benson finished.

Casey looked at her mom and a warm feeling poured over her. Her mom and Tom—and even all her friends and classmates had shown that they were behind her. Apparently, even her dad wasn't going to criticize her tonight.

That afternoon she had felt like a star and she wanted to enjoy it. She'd gone from one of the worst days of her life to one of the best!

After dinner Bear asked Casey to come into his study, saying he wanted to have a talk with her.

Casey wished she could escape. She'd needed to have this talk for weeks, but now that the moment was here, she wanted to run and hide. But she had to face him—now.

Leading the way, he went into the paneled room and struck a match to the firewood. Without speaking, he seated himself behind his desk. Casey stood in front of him, feeling a little like she'd been called to the principal's office.

Bear cleared his throat. "Your mother and Tom have mentioned that you think I'm working you too hard."

"It's not the work," she protested. "I'm used to that. It's picking at me, yelling about my mistakes in front of everybody. Do you have any idea how that makes me feel?"

"Sit down, Casey," he said softly.

She curled up in a wing chair by the fire, sure that she looked more relaxed than she felt. She willed herself to remain calm. This time they had to talk it out.

"You must know that you're one of the best." When Casey didn't answer, her dad continued. "I was sure you'd have trouble with the older girls when you made the team. Not only were you my daughter, but you were a better gymnast, too."

Casey nodded. He was right about that—she'd had trouble, all right. It was only after he'd begun treating her so poorly that the rest of the team had warmed up to the three freshmen.

"I thought I had to bend over backward to prove you weren't getting any special favors," Bear explained.

"I sure didn't get anything special. Dad, you've made my life miserable . . . almost ruined gymnastics for me," she told him.

Bear winced, and a hurt expression came into his eyes. Casey could see that he'd had no idea how awful she'd felt. "I guess I overdid it," he admitted.

"And how!" Casey muttered. "I felt so rejected . . . and so embarrassed when you kept yelling at me. I never seemed to know what you wanted from me."

"But lately your concentration *has* gone. Until today I thought you'd fallen apart."

Casey jumped to her feet. "Do you blame me? My gosh, the more I tried to please you, the worse it got. I couldn't do anything right!"

Bear rubbed his forehead, indicating that the conversation was difficult for him, too. "I've never had trouble working with any of the girls before. But you . . . my own daughter, I—"

"Tried too hard," Casey finished his sentence. Speaking softly, she said, "Do you know how many times I wanted to quit—how close I came?"

Her dad put his face in his hands for several minutes, and Casey waited. She was beginning to feel bad herself. But she wasn't going to let him off the hook. She didn't want any of this to ever happen again.

Finally, he looked up. "Can we start over?" he asked in an uncharacteristically timid voice.

"I don't know," she said slowly. "I'll stay through the season, but I don't know about next year."

"Let's just take one meet at a time, okay? I'll try to treat you the same as I treat everyone else, I honestly will. And tell me if I'm not. What do you say, sugar?"

"Okay, Dad," Casey agreed. "We can try."

A tiny smile flickered on her dad's face, and he got up and walked over to her chair. Hesitantly, he reached out and pulled her into his arms. Casey let him hug her, and wiped her teary eyes on his shirt.

Maybe they could make a fresh start. Maybe it *would* work.

Here's a look at what's ahead in BREAKING ALL THE RULES, the second book in Fawcett's "Perfect Ten" series for GIRLS ONLY.

A minute or so later, a boy who looked very familiar to Monica came sailing through the doors.

Monica had seen him before at school, she was sure of it. He was a great-looking black boy, not tall but sturdy, muscular, and powerful in build. She was almost positive that she had seen him on the boys' gymnastic team.

When he saw Monica, he stopped. "Hi," he said in a quiet, almost shy voice. He smiled tentatively, revealing straight white teeth. His dark brown eyes sparkled in the brightly lit entryway.

"Hi," Monica said in return.

"You're on the girls' gymnastic team at school," he said with quiet certainty. "You're the one who dances so beautifully on floor."

"Oh." Flustered for a moment, Monica simply stared back at him. "Thank you. How did you guess that I was in dire need of a compliment today?" she asked.

The boy threw his head back and laughed. "I didn't guess that," he said. "I was just being honest. I've seen you perform. You're incredible."

Monica was speechless. Who was this guy, anyway?

"My name is Derek Stone," he said. "And you're Monica Wright—right?" He grinned at his own silly choice of words. "Wright, right. I'll bet people do that all the time."

Monica giggled. "Only the goony ones," she joked.

"So . . . what are you doing here?" he asked. "Are you a member?"

"No," Monica said. "Are you?"

"Not me. I was just dropping off my little brother, Teddy. He's a beginner," Derek told her.

"Good for him." Monica smiled. "Well, I wish I could say I've seen you perform, but I haven't . . . yet."

Derek shrugged. "No great loss. I'm not exactly God's Gift to Fairfield High gymnastics."

"Somehow I don't believe that. You look really strong," Monica observed.

"You didn't say why you're here," Derek reminded her, changing the subject. "Just hiding indoors from the cold wind?"

"No. I thought I could get a little extra training for my bars routine. But they're all filled up. And our regular club, Flyaway, is closed for renovations. I can't believe my luck!"

Derek's brown eyes registered sympathy. They really were wonderful eyes, for a boy. Nature had given him long, thick eyelashes that Monica or any of her friends would have killed for.

"Trying to get in shape for the Carlton meet next week?" he guessed. Monica nodded. "Well, I can't help out with that problem, but I can offer you a milkshake," Derek said.

"What?" Monica looked at him, puzzled.

"A milkshake. At the dairy bar across the street. They specialize in Double Chocolate Challengers! I'm about a half hour early to pick up my brother, so I just thought we could wind down from workout together. What do you say?"

Monica realized that he was actually asking her out—sort of on a date! He was offering her a milkshake, at any rate, and the chance to sit and become better acquainted. "Make that a diet soda and you're on," she said, smiling.

Outside, the air felt warmer to Monica. The wind

didn't seem quite so harsh on her face, but she decided it was all in her head, because she was walking with a boy.

"So, tell me about your little brother, Teddy," Monica suggested as she and Derek made their way to the crosswalk at the busy intersection.

Late afternoon sun filtered through the trees, sending slender shadows onto the sidewalk. Monica felt an odd, quickened rush of blood through her veins, just walking alongside Derek. She wasn't used to being with a boy. Although she was fourteen, she'd never done any dating, and she didn't even have many boys as friends. She'd always been too busy with her gymnastics and her ballet lessons.

"My little brother?" Derek pretended to think seriously as they waited for the light to change so they could cross the street. "Let's see. What can one say about Teddy? He's a whirlwind, a human dynamo, a bundle of energy—"

Monica laughed. "And that's the reason you enrolled him in gymnastics lessons! To get him out of the house!"

"Sure. And my parents think my being in gymnastics has been good for me, too. Actually, I think they're pretty proud of me."

"My parents love the fact that I'm a gymnast, too," Monica said. "I think that's one of the things that's so rewarding about working so hard—seeing your parents' pride."

Derek turned to look at Monica. "I agree," he said quietly. Then he shook off the serious tone and grinned. "Parents!" he kidded. "You can't live with 'em and you can't live without 'em!"

"I'll drink to that," Monica said.

The traffic light changed and Derek Stone took

her hand. They crossed the street together, laughing like old friends.

Monica's heart felt much, much lighter, and she began to think that her problems would work themselves out, eventually. Meeting Derek just had to be a good omen!